PRAISE F
NEW YORK TIME
SHATTER

"Tahereh Mafi's bold, inventive prose crackles with raw
emotion. A thrilling, high-stakes saga of self-discovery and
forbidden love, the Shatter Me series is a must-read for fans
of dystopian young-adult literature—or any literature!"
—Ransom Riggs, #1 *New York Times* bestselling
author of *Miss Peregrine's Home for Peculiar Children*

"Dangerous, sexy, romantic, and intense.
I dare you to stop reading."
—Kami Garcia, #1 *New York Times* bestselling
coauthor of the Beautiful Creatures series

"Addictive, intense, and oozing with romance.
~~I'm envious.~~ I couldn't put it down."
—Lauren Kate, #1 *New York Times* bestselling
author of the Fallen series

"A gripping read from an author who's not
afraid to take risks."
—*Publishers Weekly*

"Compelling and bittersweet."
—*BCCB*

Also by Tahereh Mafi

Shatter Me

Unravel Me

Ignite Me

Destroy Me: A Shatter Me Novella

Fracture Me: A Shatter Me Novella

UNITE ME

TAHEREH MAFI

HARPER

An Imprint of HarperCollinsPublishers

Library of Congress catalog card number: 2013954354

ISBN 978-0-06-232796-3

Typography by

16 17   PC/RRDC   10 9 8

First Edition

CONTENTS

DESTROY ME

PROLOGUE

I've been shot.

And, as it turns out, a bullet wound is even more uncomfortable than I had imagined.

My skin is cold and clammy; I'm making a herculean effort to breathe. Torture is roaring through my right arm and making it difficult for me to focus. I have to squeeze my eyes shut, grit my teeth, and force myself to pay attention.

The chaos is unbearable.

Several people are shouting and too many of them are touching me, and I want their hands surgically removed. They keep shouting "Sir!" as if they're still waiting for me to give them orders, as if they have no idea what to do without my instruction. The realization exhausts me.

"Sir, can you hear me?" Another cry. But this time, a voice I don't detest.

"Sir, please, can you hear me—"

"I've been shot, Delalieu," I manage to say. I open my eyes. Look into his watery ones. "I haven't gone deaf."

All at once the noise disappears. The soldiers shut up. Delalieu looks at me. Worried.

I sigh.

"Take me back," I tell him, shifting, just a little. The

world tilts and steadies all at once. "Alert the medics and have my bed prepared for our arrival. In the meantime, elevate my arm and continue applying direct pressure to the wound. The bullet has broken or fractured something, and this will require surgery."

Delalieu says nothing for just a moment too long.

"Good to see you're all right, sir." His voice is a nervous, shaky thing. "Good to see you're all right."

"That was an order, Lieutenant."

"Of course," he says quickly, head bowed. "Certainly, sir. How should I direct the soldiers?"

"Find her," I tell him. It's getting harder for me to speak. I take a small breath and run a shaky hand across my forehead. I'm sweating in an excessive way that isn't lost on me.

"Yes, sir." He moves to help me up, but I grab his arm.

"One last thing."

"Sir?"

"Kent," I say, my voice uneven now. "Make sure they keep him alive for me."

Delalieu looks up, his eyes wide. "Private Adam Kent, sir?"

"Yes." I hold his gaze. "I want to deal with him myself."

ONE

Delalieu is standing at the foot of my bed, clipboard in hand.

His is my second visit this morning. The first was from my medics, who confirmed that the surgery went well. They said that as long as I stay in bed this week, the new drugs they've given me should accelerate my healing process. They also said that I should be fit to resume daily activities fairly soon, but I'll be required to wear a sling for at least a month.

I told them it was an interesting theory.

"My slacks, Delalieu." I'm sitting up, trying to steady my head against the nausea of these new drugs. My right arm is essentially useless to me now.

I look up. Delalieu is staring at me, unblinking, Adam's apple bobbing in his throat.

I stifle a sigh.

"What is it?" I use my left arm to steady myself against the mattress and force myself upright. It takes every ounce of energy I have left, and I'm clinging to the bed frame. I wave away Delalieu's effort to help; I close my eyes against the pain and dizziness. "Tell me what's happened," I say to him. "There's no point in prolonging bad news."

His voice breaks twice when he says, "Private Adam Kent has escaped, sir."

My eyes flash a bright, dizzying white behind my eyelids.

I take a deep breath and attempt to run my good hand through my hair. It's thick and dry and caked with what must be dirt mixed with my own blood. I'm tempted to punch my remaining fist through the wall.

Instead I take a moment to collect myself.

I'm suddenly too aware of everything in the air around me, the scents and small noises and footsteps outside my door. I hate these rough cotton pants they've put me in. I hate that I'm not wearing socks. I want to shower. I want to change.

I want to put a bullet through Adam Kent's spine.

"Leads," I demand. I move toward my bathroom and wince against the cold air as it hits my skin; I'm still without a shirt. Trying to remain calm. "Tell me you have not brought me this information without leads."

My mind is a warehouse of carefully organized human emotions. I can almost see my brain as it functions, filing thoughts and images away. I lock away the things that do not serve me. I focus only on what needs to be done: the basic components of survival and the myriad things I must manage throughout the day.

"Of course," Delalieu says. The fear in his voice stings me a little; I dismiss it. "Yes, sir," he says, "we do think we know where he might've gone—and we have reason to believe that Private Kent and the—and the girl—well, with Private Kishimoto having run off as well—we have reason to believe that they are all together, sir."

6

The drawers in my mind are rattling to break open. Memories. Theories. Whispers and sensations.

I shove them off a cliff.

"Of course you do." I shake my head. Regret it. Close my eyes against the sudden unsteadiness. "Do not give me information I've already deduced for myself," I manage to say. "I want something concrete. Give me a solid lead, Lieutenant, or leave me until you have one."

"A car," he says quickly. "A car was reported stolen, sir, and we were able to track it to an unidentified location, but then it disappeared off the map. It's as if it ceased to exist, sir."

I look up. Give him my full attention.

"We followed the tracks it left in our radar," he says, speaking more calmly now, "and they led us to a stretch of isolated, barren land. But we've scoured the area and found nothing."

"This is something, at least." I rub the back of my neck, fighting the weakness I feel deep in my bones. "I will meet you in the L Room in one hour."

"But sir," he says, eyes trained on my arm, "you'll need assistance—there's a process—you'll require a convalescent aide—"

"You are dismissed."

He hesitates.

Then, "Yes, sir."

TWO

I manage to bathe without losing consciousness.

It was more of a sponge bath, but I feel better nonetheless. I have an extremely low threshold for disorder; it offends my very being. I shower regularly. I eat six small meals a day. I dedicate two hours of each day to training and physical exercise. And I detest being barefoot.

Now, I find myself standing naked, hungry, tired, and barefoot in my closet. This is not ideal.

My closet is separated into various sections. Shirts, ties, slacks, blazers, and boots. Socks, gloves, scarves, and coats. Everything is arranged according to color, then shades within each color. Every article of clothing it contains is meticulously chosen and custom made to fit the exact measurements of my body. I don't feel like myself until I'm fully dressed; it's part of who I am and how I begin my day.

Now I haven't the faintest idea how I'm supposed to dress myself.

My hand shakes as I reach for the little blue bottle I was given this morning. I place two of the square-shaped pills on my tongue and allow them to dissolve. I'm not sure what they do; I only know they help replenish the blood I've lost. So I lean against the wall until my head clears and I feel stronger on my feet.

This, such an ordinary task. It wasn't an obstacle I was anticipating.

I put socks on first; a simple pleasure that requires more effort than shooting a man. Briefly, I wonder what the medics must've done with my clothes. *The clothes,* I tell myself, *only the clothes;* I'm focusing only on the clothes from that day. Nothing else. No other details.

Boots. Socks. Slacks. Sweater. My military jacket with its many buttons.

The many buttons she ripped open.

It's a small reminder, but it's enough to spear me.

I try to fight it off but it lingers, and the more I try to ignore the memory, it multiplies into a monster that can no longer be contained. I don't even realize I've fallen against the wall until I feel the cold climbing up my skin; I'm breathing too hard and squeezing my eyes shut against the sudden wash of mortification.

I knew she was terrified, horrified, even, but I never thought those feelings were directed toward me. I'd seen her evolve as we spent time together; she seemed more comfortable as the weeks passed. Happier. At ease. I allowed myself to believe she'd seen a future for us; that she wanted to be with me and simply thought it impossible.

I'd never suspected that her newfound happiness was a consequence of Kent.

I run my good hand down the length of my face; cover my mouth. The things I said to her.

A tight breath.

The way I touched her.

My jaw tenses.

If it were nothing but sexual attraction I'm sure I would not suffer such unbearable humiliation. But I wanted so much more than her body.

All at once I implore my mind to imagine nothing but walls. Walls. White walls. Blocks of concrete. Empty rooms. Open space.

I build walls until they begin to crumble, and then I force another set to take their place. I build and build and remain unmoving until my mind is clear, uncontaminated, containing nothing but a small white room. A single light hanging from the ceiling.

Clean. Pristine. Undisturbed.

I blink back the flood of disaster pressing against the small world I've built; I swallow hard against the fear creeping up my throat. I push the walls back, making more space in the room until I can finally breathe. Until I'm able to stand.

Sometimes I wish I could step outside of myself for a while. I want to leave this worn body behind, but my chains are too many, my weights too heavy. This life is all that's left of me. And I know I won't be able to meet myself in the mirror for the rest of the day.

I'm suddenly disgusted with myself. I have to get out of this room as soon as possible, or my own thoughts will wage war against me. I make a hasty decision and for the first time, pay little attention to what I'm wearing. I tug on a fresh pair of pants and go without a shirt. I slip my good arm into the sleeve of a blazer and allow the other shoulder to drape over the sling carrying my injured arm. I look ridiculous, exposed like this, but I'll find a solution tomorrow.

First, I have to get out of this room.

THREE

Delalieu is the only person here who does not hate me.

He still spends the majority of his time in my presence cowering in fear, but somehow he has no interest in overthrowing my position. I can feel it, though I don't understand it. He's likely the only person in this building who's pleased that I'm not dead.

I hold up a hand to keep away the soldiers who rush forward as I open my door. It takes an intense amount of concentration to keep my fingers from shaking as I wipe the slight sheen of perspiration off my forehead, but I will not allow myself a moment of weakness. These men do not fear for my safety; they only want a closer look at the spectacle I've become. They want a first look at the cracks in my sanity. But I have no wish to be wondered at.

My job is to lead.

I've been shot; it will not be fatal. There are things to be managed; I will manage them.

This wound will be forgotten.

Her name will not be spoken.

My fingers clench and unclench as I make my way toward the L Room. I never before realized just how long these corridors are and just how many soldiers line the halls. There's no reprieve from their curious stares and their disappointment that I did not die. I don't even have to look at them to know what they're thinking. But knowing how they feel only makes me more determined to live a very long life.

I will give no one the satisfaction of my death.

"No."

I wave away the tea and coffee service for the fourth time. "I do not drink caffeine, Delalieu. Why do you always insist on having it served at my meals?"

"I suppose I always hope you will change your mind, sir."

I look up. Delalieu is smiling that strange, shaky smile. And I'm not entirely certain, but I think he's just made a joke.

"Why?" I reach for a slice of bread. "I am perfectly capable of keeping my eyes open. Only an idiot would rely on the energy of a bean or a leaf to stay awake throughout the day."

Delalieu is no longer smiling.

"Yes," he says. "Certainly, sir." And stares down at his food. I watch as his fingers push away the coffee cup.

I drop the bread back onto my plate. "My opinions," I say to him, quietly this time, "should not so easily break your own. Stand by your convictions. Form clear and logical arguments. Even if I disagree."

"Of course, sir," he whispers. He says nothing for a few seconds. But then I see him reach for his coffee again.

Delalieu.

He, I think, is my only course for conversation.

13

He was originally assigned to this sector by my father, and has since been ordered to remain here until he's no longer able. And though he's likely forty-five years my senior, he insists on remaining directly below me. I've known Delalieu's face since I was a child; I used to see him around our house, sitting in on the many meetings that took place in the years before The Reestablishment took over.

There was an endless supply of meetings in my house.

My father was always planning things, leading discussions and whispered conversations I was never allowed to be a part of. The men of those meetings are running this world now, so when I look at Delalieu I can't help but wonder why he never aspired to more. He was a part of this regime from the very beginning, but somehow seems content to die just as he is now. He chooses to remain subservient, even when I give him opportunities to speak up; he refuses to be promoted, even when I offer him higher pay. And while I appreciate his loyalty, his dedication unnerves me. He does not seem to wish for more than what he has.

I should not trust him.

And yet, I do.

But I've begun to lose my mind for a lack of companionable conversation. I cannot maintain anything but a cool distance from my soldiers, not only because they all wish to see me dead, but also because I have a responsibility as their leader to make unbiased decisions. I have sentenced myself to a life of solitude, one wherein I have no peers, and no mind but my own to live in. I looked to build myself as a feared leader, and I've succeeded; no one will question my authority or posit a contrary opinion. No one will speak to me as anything but the chief commander and regent of Sector 45. Friendship is not a thing I have ever experienced. Not as a child, and not as I am now.

Except.

One month ago, I met the exception to this rule. There *has* been one person who's ever looked me directly in the eye. The same person who's spoken to me with no filter; someone who's been unafraid to show anger and real, raw feeling in my presence; the only one who's ever dared to challenge me, to raise her voice to me—

I squeeze my eyes shut for what feels like the tenth time today. I unclench my fist around this fork, drop it to the table. My arm has begun to throb again, and I reach for the pills tucked away in my pocket.

"You shouldn't take more than eight of those within a twenty-four-hour period, sir."

I open the cap and toss three more into my mouth. I really wish my hands would stop shaking. My muscles feel too tight, too tense. Stretched thin.

I don't wait for the pills to dissolve. I bite down on them, crunching against their bitterness. There's something about the foul, metallic taste that helps me focus. "Tell me about Kent."

Delalieu knocks over his coffee cup.

The dining aides have left the room at my request; Delalieu receives no assistance as he scrambles to clean up the mess. I sit back in my chair, staring at the wall just behind him, mentally tallying up the minutes I've lost today.

"Leave the coffee."

"I—yes, of course, sorry, sir—"

"Stop."

Delalieu drops the sopping napkins. His hands are frozen in place, hovering over his plate.

"Speak."

I watch his throat move as he swallows, hesitates. "We don't know, sir," he whispers. "The building should've been impossible to find, much less to enter. It'd been bolted and rusted shut. But when we found it," he says, "when we found it, it was . . . the door had been destroyed. And we're not sure how they managed it."

I sit up. "What do you mean, *destroyed*?"

He shakes his head. "It was . . . very odd, sir. The door had been . . . mangled. As if some kind of animal had clawed through it. There was only a gaping, ragged hole in the middle of the frame."

I stand up entirely too fast, gripping the table for support. I'm breathless at the thought of it, at the possibility of what must've happened. And I can't help but allow myself the painful pleasure of recalling her name once more, because I know it must've been her. She must've done something extraordinary, and I wasn't even there to witness it.

16

"Call for transport," I tell him. "I will meet you in the Quadrant in exactly ten minutes."

"Sir?"

I'm already out the door.

FOUR

Clawed through the middle. Just like an animal. It's true.

To an unsuspecting observer it would be the only explanation, but even then it wouldn't make any sense. No animal
alive could claw through this many inches of reinforced steel
without amputating its own limbs.

And she is not an animal.

She is a soft, deadly creature. Kind and timid and terrifying. She's completely out of control and has no idea what
she's capable of. And even though she hates me, I can't help
but be fascinated by her. I'm enchanted by her pretend-inno-
cence; jealous, even, of the power she wields so unwittingly.
I want so much to be a part of her world. I want to know
what it's like to be in her mind, to feel what she feels. It
seems a tremendous weight to carry.

And now she's out there, somewhere, unleashed on society.

What a beautiful disaster.

I run my fingers along the jagged edges of the hole,
careful not to cut myself. There's no design to it, no premed-
itation. Only an anguished fervor so readily apparent in the
chaotic ripping-apart of this door. I can't help but wonder
if she knew what she was doing when this happened, or if

it was just as unexpected to her as it was the day she broke through that concrete wall to get to me.

I have to stifle a smile. I wonder how she must remember that day. Every soldier I've worked with has walked into a simulation knowing exactly what to expect, but I purposely kept those details from her. I thought the experience should be as undiluted as possible; I hoped the spare, realistic elements would lend authenticity to the event. More than anything else, I wanted her to have a chance to explore her true nature—to exercise her strength in a safe space—and given her past, I knew a child would be the perfect trigger. But I never could've anticipated such revolutionary results. Her performance was more than I had hoped for. And though I wanted to discuss the effects with her afterward, by the time I found her she was already planning her escape.

My smile falters.

"Would you like to step inside, sir?" Delalieu's voice jolts me back to the present. "There's not much to see within, but it is interesting to note that the hole is just big enough for someone to easily climb through. It seems clear, sir, what the intent was."

I nod, distracted. My eyes carefully catalog the dimensions of the hole; I try to imagine what it must've been like for her, to be here, trying to get through. I want so much to be able to talk to her about all of this.

My heart twists so suddenly.

I'm reminded, all over again, that she's no longer with me. She does not live on base anymore.

It's my fault she's gone. I allowed myself to believe she was finally doing well and it affected my judgment. I should've been paying closer attention to details. To my soldiers. I lost sight of my purpose and my greater goal; the entire reason I brought her on base. I was stupid. Careless.

But the truth is, I was distracted.

By her.

She was so stubborn and childish when she first arrived, but as the weeks passed she'd seemed to settle; she felt less anxious to me, somehow less afraid. I have to keep reminding myself that her improvements had nothing to do with me.

They had to do with Kent.

A betrayal that somehow seemed impossible. That she would leave me for a robotic, unfeeling idiot like Kent. His thoughts are so empty, so mindless; it's like conversing with a desk lamp. I don't understand what he could've offered her, what she could've possibly seen in him except a tool for escape.

She still hasn't grasped that there's no future for her in the world of common people. She doesn't belong in the company of those who will never understand her. And I have to get her back.

I only realize I've said that last bit out loud when Delalieu speaks.

"We have troops all across the sector searching for her," he says. "And we've alerted the neighboring sectors, just in case the group of them should cross ove—"

"What?" I spin around, my voice a quiet, dangerous thing. "What did you just say?"

Delalieu has turned a sickly shade of white.

"I was unconscious for all of one night! And you've already alerted the other sectors to this *catastrophe*—"

"I thought you would want to find them, sir, and I thought, if they should try to seek refuge elsewhere—"

I take a moment to breathe, to gather my bearings.

"I'm sorry, sir, I thought it would be safest—"

"She is with two of my own soldiers, Lieutenant. Neither one of them are stupid enough to guide her toward another sector. They have neither the clearance nor the tools to obtain said clearance in order to cross the sector line."

"But—"

"They've been gone one day. They are badly wounded and in need of aid. They're traveling on foot and with a stolen vehicle that is easily trackable. How far," I say to him, frustration breaking into my voice, "could they have gone?"

Delalieu says nothing.

"You have sent out a national alert. You've notified multiple sectors, which means the entire country now knows. Which means the capitals have received word. Which means what?" I curl my only working hand into a fist. "What do you think that means, Lieutenant?"

For a moment, he seems unable to speak.

Then

"Sir," he gasps. "Please forgive me."

FIVE

Delalieu follows me to my door.

"Gather the troops in the Quadrant tomorrow at ten hundred hours," I say to him by way of good-bye. "I'll have to make an announcement about these recent events as well as what's to come."

"Yes, sir," Delalieu says. He doesn't look up. He hasn't looked at me since we left the warehouse.

I have other matters to worry about.

Not counting Delalieu's stupidity, there are an infinite number of things I must take care of right now. I can't afford any more difficulties, and I cannot be distracted. Not by her. Not by Delalieu. Not by anyone. I have to focus.

This is a terrible time to be wounded.

News of our situation has already hit a national level. Civilians and neighboring sectors are now aware of our minor uprising, and we have to tamp down the rumors as much as possible. I have to somehow defuse the alerts Delalieu has already sent out, and simultaneously suppress any hope of rebellion among the citizens. They're already too eager to resist, and any spark of controversy will reignite their fervor. Too many have died already, and they still don't seem to understand that standing against The Reestablishment is asking for more destruction. The civilians *must* be pacified.

I do not want war in my sector.

Now more than ever, I need to be in control of myself and my responsibilities. But my mind is scattered, my body fatigued and wounded. All day I've been inches from collapsing, and I don't know what to do. I have no idea how to fix it. This weakness is foreign to my being.

In just two days, one girl has managed to cripple me.

I've taken even more of these disgusting pills, but I feel weaker than I did this morning. I thought I could ignore the pain and inconvenience of a wounded shoulder, but the complication refuses to diminish. I am now wholly dependent on whatever will carry me through these next weeks of frustration. Medicine, medics, hours in bed.

All this for a kiss.

It's almost unbearable.

"I'll be in my office for the rest of the day," I tell Delalieu. "Have my meals sent to my room, and do not disturb me unless there are any new developments."

"Yes, sir."

"That'll be all, Lieutenant."

"Yes, sir."

I don't even realize how ill I feel until I close the bedroom door behind me. I stagger to the bed and grip the frame to keep from falling over. I'm sweating again and decide to strip the extra coat I wore on our outside excursion. I yank off the blazer I'd carelessly tossed over my injured shoulder this morning and fall backward onto my bed. I'm suddenly freezing. My good hand shakes as I reach for the medic call button.

I need to get the dressing on my shoulder changed. I need to eat something substantial. And more than anything else, I desperately need to take a real shower, which seems altogether impossible.

Someone is standing over me.

I blink several times but can only make out the general outline of their figure. A face keeps coming in and out of focus until I finally give up. My eyes fall closed. My head is pounding. Pain is searing through my bones and up my neck; reds and yellows and blues blur together behind my eyelids. I catch only clips of the conversation around me.

—seems to have developed a fever—

—probably sedate him—

—how many did he take?—

They're going to kill me, I realize. This is the perfect opportunity. I'm weak and unable to fight back, and someone has finally come to kill me. This is it. My moment. It has arrived. And somehow I can't seem to accept it.

I take a swipe at the voices; an inhuman sound escapes my throat. Something hard hits my fist and crashes to the floor. Hands clamp down on my right arm and pin it in place. Something is being tightened around my ankles, my wrist. I'm thrashing against these new restraints and kicking desperately at the air. The blackness seems to be pressing against my eyes, my ears, my throat. I can't breathe, can't hear or see clearly, and the suffocation of the moment is so terrifying that I'm almost certain I've lost my mind.

Something cold and sharp pinches my arm.

I have only a moment to reflect on the pain before it engulfs me.

SIX

"Juliette," I whisper. "What are you doing here?"

I'm half-dressed, getting ready for my day, and it's too early for visitors. These hours just before the sun rises are my only moments of peace, and no one should be in here. It seems impossible she gained access to my private quarters.

Someone should've stopped her.

Instead, she's standing in my doorway, staring at me. I've seen her so many times, but this is different—it's causing me physical pain to look at her. But somehow I still find myself drawn to her, wanting to be near her.

"I'm so sorry," she says, and she's wringing her hands, looking away from me. "I'm so, so sorry."

I notice what she's wearing.

It's a dark-green dress with fitted sleeves; a simple cut made of stretch cotton that clings to the soft curves of her figure. It complements the flecks of green in her eyes in a way I couldn't have anticipated. It's one of the many dresses I chose for her. I thought she might enjoy having something nice after being caged as an animal for so long. And I can't quite explain it, but it gives me a strange sense of pride to see her wearing something I picked out myself.

"I'm sorry," she says for the third time.

I'm again struck by how impossible it is that she's here. In my bedroom. Staring at me without my shirt on. Her hair is so long it falls to the middle of her back; I have to clench my fists against this unbidden need to run my hands through it. She's so beautiful.

I don't understand why she keeps apologizing.

She shuts the door behind her. She's walking over to me. My heart is beating quickly now, and it doesn't feel natural. I do not react this way. I do not lose control. I see her every day and manage to maintain some semblance of dignity, but something is off; this isn't right.

She's touching my arm.

She's running her fingers along the curve of my shoulder, and the brush of her skin against mine is making me want to scream. The pain is excruciating, but I can't speak; I'm frozen in place.

I want to tell her to stop, to leave, but parts of me are at war. I'm happy to have her close even if it hurts, even if it doesn't make any sense. But I can't seem to reach for her; I can't hold her like I've always wanted to.

She looks at me.

She searches me with those odd, blue-green eyes and I feel guilty so suddenly, without understanding why. But there's something about the way she looks at me that always makes me feel insignificant, as if she's the only one who's realized I'm entirely hollow inside. She's found the cracks in this cast I'm forced to wear every day, and it petrifies me.

That this girl would know exactly how to shatter me.

She rests her hand against my collarbone.

And then she grips my shoulder, digs her fingers into my skin like she's trying to tear off my arm. The agony is so blinding that this time I actually scream. I fall to my knees before her and she wrenches my arm, twisting it backward until I'm heaving from the effort to stay calm, fighting not to lose myself to the pain.

"Juliette," I gasp, "please—"

She runs her free hand through my hair, tugs my head back so I'm forced to meet her eyes. And then she leans into my ear, her lips almost touching my cheek. "Do you love me?" she whispers.

"What?" I breathe. "What are you doing—"

"Do you still love me?" she asks again, her fingers now tracing the shape of my face, the line of my jaw.

"Yes," I tell her. "Yes I still do—"

She smiles.

It's such a sweet, innocent smile that I'm actually shocked when her grip tightens around my arm. She twists my shoulder back until I'm sure it's being ripped from the socket. I'm seeing spots when she says, "It's almost over now."

"What is?" I ask, frantic, trying to look around. "What's almost over—"

"Just a little longer and I'll leave."

"No—no, don't go—where are you going—"

"You'll be all right," she says. "I promise."

"No," I'm gasping, "no—"

28

All at once she yanks me forward, and I'm awake so quickly I can't breathe.

I blink several times only to realize I've woken up in the middle of the night. Absolute blackness greets me from the corners of my room. My chest is heaving; my arm is bound and pounding, and I realize my pain medication has worn off. There's a small remote wedged under my hand; I press the button to replenish the dosage.

It takes a few moments for my breathing to stabilize. My thoughts slowly retreat from panic.

Juliette.

I can't control a nightmare, but in my waking moments her name is the only reminder I will permit myself.

The accompanying humiliation will not allow me much more than that.

SEVEN

"Well, isn't this embarrassing. My son, tied down like an animal."

I'm half-convinced I'm having another nightmare. I blink my eyes open slowly; I stare up at the ceiling. I make no sudden movements, but I can feel the very real weight of restraints around my left wrist and both ankles. My injured arm is still bound and slung across my chest. And though the pain in my shoulder is present, it's dulled to a light hum. I feel stronger. Even my head feels clearer, sharper somehow. But then I taste the tang of something sour and metal in my mouth and wonder how long I've been in bed.

"Did you really think I wouldn't find out?" he asks, amused.

He moves closer to my bed, his footsteps reverberating right through me. "You have Delalieu whimpering apologies for disturbing me, begging my men to blame him for the inconvenience of this unexpected visit. No doubt you terrified the old man for doing his job, when the truth is, I would've found out even without his alerts. This," he says, "is not the kind of mess you can conceal. You're an idiot for thinking otherwise."

I feel a light tugging on my legs and realize he's undoing

my restraints. The brush of his skin against mine is abrupt and unexpected, and it triggers something deep and dark within me, enough to make me physically ill. I taste vomit at the back of my throat. It takes all my self-control not to jerk away from him.

"Sit up, son. You should be well enough to function now. You were too stupid to rest when you were supposed to, and now you've overcorrected. Three days you've been unconscious, and I arrived twenty-seven hours ago. Now get up. This is ridiculous."

I'm still staring at the ceiling. Hardly breathing.

He changes tactics.

"You know," he says carefully, "I've actually heard an interesting story about you." He sits down on the edge of my bed; the mattress creaks and groans under his weight. "Would you like to hear it?"

My left hand has begun to tremble. I clench it fast against the bedsheets.

"Private 45B-76423. Fletcher, Seamus." He pauses. "Does that name sound familiar?"

I squeeze my eyes shut.

"Imagine my surprise," he says, "when I heard that my son had finally done something right. That he'd finally taken initiative and dispensed with a traitorous soldier who'd been stealing from our storage compounds. I heard you shot him right in the forehead." A laugh. "I congratulated myself— told myself you'd finally come into your own, that you'd finally learned how to lead properly. I was almost proud.

"That's why it came as an even greater shock to me to hear Fletcher's family was still alive." He claps his hands together. "Shocking, of course, because you, of all people, should know the rules. Traitors come from a family of traitors, and one betrayal means death to them all."

He rests his hand on my chest.

I'm building walls in my mind again. White walls. Blocks of concrete. Empty rooms and open space.

Nothing exists inside of me. Nothing stays.

"It's funny," he continues, thoughtful now, "because I told myself I'd wait to discuss this with you. But somehow, *this* moment seems so right, doesn't it?" I can hear him smile. "To tell you just how tremendously . . . *disappointed* I am. Though I can't say I'm surprised." He sighs. "In a single month you've lost two soldiers, couldn't contain a clinically insane girl, upended an entire sector, and encouraged rebellion among the citizens. And somehow, I'm not surprised at all."

His hand shifts; lingers at my collarbone.

White walls, I think.

Blocks of concrete.

Empty rooms. Open space.

Nothing exists inside of me. Nothing stays.

"But what's worse than all this," he says, "is not that you've managed to humiliate me by disrupting the order I'd finally managed to establish. It's not even that you somehow got yourself shot in the process. But that you would show sympathy to the family of a *traitor*," he says, laughing, his voice a happy, cheerful thing. "This is unforgivable."

My eyes are open now, blinking up at the fluorescent lights above my head, focused on the white of the bulbs blurring my vision. I will not move. I will not speak.

His hand closes around my throat.

The movement is so rough and violent I'm almost relieved. Some part of me always hopes he'll go through with it; that maybe this time he'll actually let me die. But he never does. It never lasts.

Torture is not torture when there's any hope of relief.

He lets go all too soon and gets exactly what he wants. I jerk upward, coughing and wheezing and finally making a sound that acknowledges his existence in this room. My whole body is shaking now, my muscles in shock from the assault and from remaining still for so long. My skin is cold sweat; my breaths are labored and painful.

"You're very lucky," he says, his words too soft. He's up now, no longer inches from my face. "So lucky I was here to make things right. So lucky I had time to correct the mistake."

I freeze.

The room spins.

"I was able to track down his wife," he says. "Fletcher's wife and their three children. I hear they sent their regards." A pause. "Well, this was before I had them killed, so I suppose it doesn't really matter now, but my men told me they said hello. It seems she remembered you," he says, laughing softly. "The wife. She said you went to visit them before all this . . . unpleasantness occurred. You were always visiting the compounds, she said. Asking after the civilians."

I whisper the only two words I can manage.

"Get out."

"This is my boy!" he says, waving a hand in my direction. "A meek, pathetic fool. Some days I'm so disgusted by you I don't know whether to shoot you myself. And then I realize you'd probably like that, wouldn't you? To be able to blame me for your downfall? And I think no, best to let him die of his own stupidity."

I stare blankly ahead, fingers flexing against the mattress.

"Now tell me," he says, "what happened to your arm? Delalieu seemed as clueless as the others."

I say nothing.

"Too ashamed to admit you were shot by one of your own soldiers, then?"

I close my eyes.

"And what about the girl?" he asks. "How did she escape? Ran off with one of your men, didn't she?"

I grip the bedsheet so hard my fist starts shaking.

"Tell me," he says, leaning into my ear. "How would you deal with a traitor like that? Are you going to go visit his family, too? Make nice with his wife?"

And I don't mean to say it out loud, but I can't stop myself in time. "I'm going to kill him."

He laughs out loud so suddenly it's almost a howl. He claps a hand on my head and musses my hair with the same fingers he just closed around my throat. "Much better," he says. "So much better. Now get up. We have work to do."

And I think yes, I wouldn't mind doing the kind of work that would remove Adam Kent from this world.

A traitor like him does not deserve to live.

EIGHT

I'm in the shower for so long I actually lose track of time.

This has never happened before.

Everything is off, unbalanced. I'm second-guessing my decisions, doubting everything I thought I didn't believe in, and for the first time in my life, I am genuinely, bone-achingly tired.

My father is here.

We are sleeping under the same godforsaken roof; a thing I'd hoped never to experience again. But he's here, staying on base in his own private quarters until he feels confident enough to leave. Which means he'll be fixing our problems by wreaking havoc on Sector 45. Which means I will be reduced to becoming his puppet and messenger, because my father never shows his face to anyone except those he's about to kill.

He is the supreme commander of The Reestablishment, and prefers to dictate anonymously. He travels everywhere with the same select group of soldiers, communicates only through his men, and only in extremely rare circumstances does he ever leave the capital.

News of his arrival at Sector 45 has probably spread around base by now, and has likely terrified my soldiers.

Because his presence, real or imagined, has only ever signified one thing: torture.

It's been so long since I've felt like a coward.

But this, this is bliss. This protracted moment—this illusion—of strength. Being out of bed and able to bathe: it's a small victory. The medics wrapped my injured arm in some kind of impermeable plastic for the shower, and I'm finally well enough to stand on my own. My nausea has settled, the dizziness is gone. I should finally be able to think clearly, and yet, my choices still seem so muddled.

I've forced myself not to think about her, but I'm beginning to realize I'm still not strong enough; not just yet, and especially not while I'm still actively searching for her. It's become a physical impossibility.

Today, I need to go back to her room.

I need to search her things for any clues that might help me find her. Kent's and Kishimoto's bunks and lockers have already been cleared out; nothing incriminating was found. But I'd ordered my men to leave her room—*Juliette's* room—exactly as it was. No one but myself is allowed to reenter that space. Not until I've had the first look.

And this, according to my father, is my first task.

"That'll be all, Delalieu. I'll let you know if I require assistance."

He's been following me around even more than usual lately. Apparently he came to check on me when I didn't show for the assembly I'd called two days ago, and had the pleasure of finding me completely delirious and half out of my mind. He's somehow managed to lay the blame for all this on himself.

If he were anyone else, I would've had him demoted.

"Yes, sir. I'm sorry, sir. And please forgive me—I never meant to cause additional problems—"

"You are in no danger from me, Lieutenant."

"I'm so sorry, sir," he whispers. His shoulders fall. His head bows.

His apologies are making me uncomfortable. "Have the troops reassemble at thirteen hundred hours. I still need to address them about these recent developments."

"Yes, sir," he says. He nods once, without looking up.

"You are dismissed."

"Sir." He drops his salute and disappears.

I'm left alone in front of her door.

Funny, how accustomed I'd become to visiting her here; how it gave me a strange sense of comfort to know that she and I were living in the same building. Her presence on base changed everything for me; the weeks she spent here became the first I ever enjoyed living in these quarters. I looked forward to her temper. Her tantrums. Her ridiculous arguments. I wanted her to yell at me; I would've congratulated her had she ever slapped me in the face. I was always pushing her, toying with her emotions. I wanted to meet the real girl trapped behind the fear. I wanted her to finally break free of her own carefully constructed restraints.

Because while she might be able to feign timidity within the confines of isolation, out here—amid chaos, destruction—I knew she'd become something entirely different. I was just waiting. Every day, patiently waiting for her to understand the breadth of her own potential; never realizing I'd entrusted her to the one soldier who might take her away from me.

I should shoot myself for it.

Instead, I open the door.

The panel slides shut behind me as I cross the threshold. I find myself alone, standing here, in the last place she touched. The bed is messy and unmade, the doors to her armoire hanging open, the broken window temporarily taped shut. There's a sinking, nervous pain in my stomach that I choose to ignore.

Focus.

I step into the bathroom and examine the toiletries, the cabinets, even the inside of the shower.

Nothing.

I walk back over to the bed and run my hand over the rumpled comforter, the lumpy pillows. I allow myself a moment to appreciate the evidence that she was once here, and then I strip the bed. Sheets, pillowcases, comforter, and duvet; all tossed to the floor. I scrutinize every inch of the pillows, the mattress, and the bed frame, and again find nothing.

The side table. Nothing.

Under the bed. Nothing.

The light fixtures, the wallpaper, each individual piece of clothing in her armoire. Nothing.

It's only as I'm making my way toward the door that something catches my foot. I look down. There, caught just under my boot, is a thick, faded rectangle. A small, unassuming notebook that could fit in the palm of my hand.

And I'm so stunned that for a moment I can't even move.

NINE

How could I have forgotten?

This notebook was in her pocket the day she was making her escape. I'd found it just before Kent put a gun to my head, and at some point in the chaos, I must've dropped it. And I realize I should've been looking for this all along.

I bend down to pick it up, carefully shaking out bits and pieces of glass from the pages. My hand is unsteady, my heart pounding in my ears. I have no idea what this might contain. Pictures. Notes. Scrambled, half-formed thoughts.

It could be anything.

I flip the notebook over in my hands, my fingers memorizing its rough, worn surface. The cover is a dull shade of brown, but I can't tell if it's been stained by dirt and age, or if it was always this color. I wonder how long she's had it. Where she might've acquired it.

I stumble backward, the backs of my legs hitting her bed. My knees buckle, and I catch myself on the edge of the mattress. I take in a shaky breath and close my eyes.

I'd seen footage from her time in the asylum, but it was essentially useless. The lighting was always too dim; the small window did little to illuminate the dark corners of her room. She was often an indistinguishable form; a dark shadow one might never even notice. Our cameras were only good at detecting movement—and maybe a lucky moment when the sun hit her at the right angle—but she rarely moved. Most of her time was spent sitting very, very still, on her bed or in a dark corner. She almost never spoke. And when she did, it was never in words. She spoke only in numbers.

Counting.

There was something so unreal about her, sitting there. I couldn't even see her face; couldn't discern the outline of her figure. Even then she fascinated me. That she could seem so calm, so still. She would sit in one place for hours at a time, unmoving, and I always wondered where she was in her mind, what she might be thinking, how she could possibly exist in that solitary world. More than anything else, I wanted to hear her speak.

I was desperate to hear her voice.

I'd always expected her to speak in a language I could understand. I thought she'd start with something simple. Maybe something unintelligible. But the first time we ever caught her talking on camera, I couldn't look away. I sat there, transfixed, nerves stretched thin, as she touched one hand to the wall and counted.

4,572.

I watched her count. To 4,572.

It took five hours.

Only afterward did I realize she was counting her breaths.

I couldn't stop thinking about her after that. I was distracted long before she arrived on base, constantly wondering what she might be doing and whether she'd speak again. If she wasn't counting out loud, was she counting in her head? Did she ever think in letters? Complete sentences? Was she angry? Sad? Why did she seem so serene for a girl I'd been told was a volatile, deranged animal? Was it a trick?

I'd seen every piece of paper documenting the critical moments in her life. I'd read every detail in her medical records and police reports; I'd sorted through school complaints, doctors' notes, her official sentencing by The Reestablishment, and even the asylum questionnaire submitted by her parents. I knew she'd been pulled out of school at fourteen. I knew she'd been through severe testing and was forced to take various—and dangerous—experimental drugs, and had to undergo electroshock therapy. In two years she'd been in and out of nine different juvenile detention centers and had been examined by more than fifty different doctors. All of them described her as a monster. They called her a danger to society and a threat to humanity. A girl who would ruin our world and had already begun by murdering a small child. At sixteen, her parents suggested she be locked away. And so she was.

None of it made sense to me.

A girl cast off by society, by her own family—she had to contain so much feeling. Rage. Depression. Resentment. Where was it?

She was nothing like the other inmates at the asylum—the

43

ones who were truly disturbed. Some would spend hours hurling themselves at the wall, breaking bones and fracturing skulls. Others were so deranged they would claw at their own skin until they drew blood, literally ripping themselves to pieces. Some had entire conversations with themselves out loud, laughing and singing and arguing. Most would tear their clothes off, content to sleep and stand naked in their own filth. She was the only one who showered regularly or even washed her clothes. She would take her meals calmly, always finishing whatever she was given. And she spent most of her time staring out the window.

She'd been locked up for almost a year and had not lost her sense of humanity. I wanted to know how she could suppress so much; how she'd achieved such outward calm. I'd asked for profiles on the other prisoners because I wanted comparisons. I wanted to know if her behavior was normal.

It wasn't.

I watched the unassuming outline of this girl I could not see and did not know, and I felt an unbelievable amount of respect for her. I admired her, envied her composure—her steadiness in the face of all she'd been forced to endure. I don't know that I understood what it was, exactly, I was feeling at the time, but I knew I wanted her all to myself.

I wanted to know her secrets.

And then one day, she stood up in her cell and walked over to the window. It was early morning, just as the sun was rising; I caught a glimpse of her face for the very first time. She pressed her palm to the window and whispered two words, just once.

Forgive me.

I hit rewind too many times.

I could never tell anyone I'd developed a newfound fascination with her. I had to effect a pretense, an outward indifference—an arrogance—toward her. She was to be our weapon and nothing more, just an innovative instrument of torture.

A detail I cared very little about.

My research had led me to her files by pure accident. Coincidence. I did not seek her out in search of a weapon; I never had. Far before I'd ever seen her on film, and far, far before I ever spoke a word to her, I had been researching something else. For something else.

My motives were my own.

Utilizing her as a weapon was a story I fed to my father; I needed an excuse to have access to her, to gain the necessary clearance to study her files. It was a charade I was forced to maintain in front of my soldiers and the hundreds of cameras that monitor my existence. I did not bring her on base to exploit her ability. And I certainly did not expect to fall for her in the process.

But these truths and my real motivations will be buried with me.

I fall hard onto the bed. Clap a hand over my forehead, drag it down the length of my face. I never would've sent

Kent to stay with her if I could've taken the time to go myself. Every move I made was a mistake. Every calculated effort was a failure. I only wanted to watch her interact with someone. I wondered if she'd seem different; if she'd shatter the expectations I'd already formed in my mind by simply having a normal conversation. But watching her talk to someone else made me crazy. I was jealous. Ridiculous. I wanted her to know *me*; I wanted her to talk to *me*. And I felt it then: this strange, inexplicable sense that she might be the only person in the world I could really care about.

I force myself to sit up. I hazard a glance at the notebook still clutched in my hand.

I lost her.

She hates me.

She hates me and I repulse her and I might never see her again, and it is entirely my own doing. This notebook might be all I have left of her. My hand is still hovering over the cover, tempting me to open it and find her again, even if it's only for a short while, even if it's only on paper. But part of me is terrified. This might not end well. This might not be anything I want to see. And so help me, if this turns out to be some kind of diary concerning her thoughts and feelings about Kent, I might just throw myself out the window.

I pound my fist against my forehead. Take a long, steadying breath.

Finally, I flip it open. My eyes fall to the first page.

And only then do I begin to understand the weight of what I've found.

I keep thinking I need to stay calm, that it's all in my head, that everything is going to be fine and someone is going to open the door now, someone is going to let me out of here. I keep thinking it's going to happen. I keep thinking it has to happen, because things like this don't just happen. This doesn't happen. People aren't forgotten like this. Not abandoned like this.

This doesn't just happen.

My face is caked with blood from when they threw me on the ground, and my hands are still shaking even as I write this. This pen is my only outlet, my only voice, because I have no one else to speak to, no mind but my own to drown in and all the lifeboats are taken and all the life preservers are broken and I don't know how to swim I can't swim I can't swim and it's getting so hard. It's getting so hard. It's like there are a million screams caught inside of my chest but I have to keep them all in because what's the point of screaming if you'll never be heard and no one will ever hear me in here. No one will ever hear me again.

I've learned to stare at things.

The walls. My hands. The cracks in the walls. The lines on my fingers. The shades of gray in the concrete. The shape of my fingernails. I pick one thing and stare at it for what must be hours. I keep time in my head by counting the seconds as they pass. I keep days in my head by writing them down. Today is day two. Today is the second day. Today is a day.

Today.

It's so cold. It's so cold it's so cold.

Please please please

I slam the cover shut.

I'm shaking again, and this time I can't stop it. This time the shaking is coming from deep within my core, from a profound realization of what I'm holding in my hands. This journal is not from her time spent here. It has nothing to do with me, or Kent, or anyone at all. This journal is a documentation of her days spent in the asylum.

And suddenly this small, battered notebook means more to me than anything I've ever owned.

TEN

I don't even know how I manage to get myself back to my own rooms so quickly. All I know is that I've locked the door to my bedroom, unlocked the door to my office only to lock myself inside, and now I'm sitting here, at my desk, stacks of papers and confidential material shoved out of the way, staring at the tattered cover of something I'm very nearly terrified to read. There's something so personal about this journal; it looks as if it's been bound together by the loneliest feelings, the most vulnerable moments of one person's life. She wrote whatever lies within these pages during some of the darkest hours of her seventeen years, and I'm about to get exactly what I've always wanted.

A look into her mind.

And though the anticipation is killing me, I'm also acutely aware of just how badly this might backfire. I'm suddenly not sure I even want to know. And yet I do. I definitely do.

So I open the book, and turn to the next page. Day three.

I started screaming today.

And those four words hit me harder than the worst kind of physical pain.

My chest is rising and falling, my breaths coming in too hard. I have to force myself to keep reading.

I soon realize there's no order to the pages. She seems to have started back at the beginning after she came to the end of the notebook and realized she'd run out of space. She's written in the margins, over other paragraphs, in tiny and nearly illegible fonts. There are numbers scrawled all over everything, sometimes the same number repeating over and over and over again. Sometimes the same word has been written and rewritten, circled and underlined. And nearly every page has sentences and paragraphs almost entirely crossed out.

It's complete chaos.

My heart constricts at this realization, at this proof of what she must've experienced. I'd hypothesized about what she might've suffered in all that time, locked up in such dark, horrifying conditions. But seeing it for myself—I wish I weren't right.

And now, even as I try to read in chronological order, I find I'm unable to keep up with the method she's used to number everything; the system she created on these pages is something only she'd be able to decipher. I can only flip through the book and seek out the bits that are most coherently written.

My eyes freeze on a particular passage.

It's a strange thing, to never know peace. To know that no matter where you go, there is no sanctuary. That the threat of pain is always a whisper away. I'm not safe locked into these 4 walls, I was never safe leaving my house, and I couldn't even feel safe in the 14 years I lived at home. The asylum kills people every day, the world has already been taught to fear me, and my home is the same place where my father locked me in my room every night and my mother screamed at me for being the abomination she was forced to raise.

She always said it was my face.

There was something about my face, she said, that she couldn't stand. Something about my eyes, the way I looked at her, the fact that I even existed. She'd always tell me to stop looking at her. She'd always scream it. Like I might attack her. Stop looking at me, she'd scream. You just stop looking at me, she'd scream.

She put my hand in the fire once.

Just to see if it would burn, she said. Just to check if it was a regular hand, she said.

I was 6 years old then.

I remember because it was my birthday.

I knock the notebook to the floor.

I'm upright in an instant, trying to steady my heart. I run a hand through my hair, my fingers caught at the roots. These words are too close to me, too familiar. The story of a child abused by its parents. Locked away and discarded. It's too close to my mind.

I've never read anything like this before. I've never read anything that could speak directly to my bones. And I know I shouldn't. I know, somehow, that it won't help, that it won't teach me anything, that it won't give me clues about where she might've gone. I already know that reading this will only make me crazy.

But I can't stop myself from reaching for her journal once more.

I flip it open again.

> ~~Am I insane yet?~~
> ~~Has it happened yet?~~
> ~~How will I ever know?~~

My intercom screeches so suddenly that I trip over my own chair and have to catch myself on the wall behind my desk. My hands won't stop shaking; my forehead is beaded with sweat. My bandaged arm has begun to burn, and my legs are suddenly too weak to stand on. I have to focus all my energy on sounding normal as I accept the incoming message.

"What?" I demand.

"Sir, I only wondered, if you were still—well, the assembly, sir, unless of course I got the time wrong, I'm so sorry, I shouldn't have bothered you—"

"Oh for the love of God, Delalieu." I try to shake off the

tremble in my voice. "Stop apologizing. I'm on my way."

"Yes, sir," he says. "Thank you, sir."

I disconnect the line.

And then I grab the notebook, tuck it in my pocket, and head out the door.

ELEVEN

I'm standing at the edge of the courtyard above the Quadrant, looking out at the thousands of faces staring back at me. These are my soldiers. Standing single-file line in their assembly uniforms. Black shirts, black pants, black boots.

No guns.

Left fists pressed against their hearts.

I make an effort to focus on—and care about—the task at hand; but somehow I can't help but be hyperaware of the notebook tucked away in my pocket, the shape of it pressing against my leg and torturing me with its secrets.

I am not myself.

My thoughts are tangled in words that are not my own. I have to take a sharp breath to clear my head; I clench and unclench my fist.

"Sector 45," I say, speaking directly into the square of microphonic mesh.

They shift at once, dropping their left hands and instead placing their right fists on their chests.

"We have a number of important things to discuss today," I tell them, "the first of which is readily apparent." I gesture to my arm. Study their carefully crafted emotionless faces.

Their traitorous thoughts are so obvious.

They think of me as little more than a deranged child. They do not respect me; they are not loyal to me. They are disappointed that I stand before them; angry; disgusted, even, that I am not dead of this wound.

But they do fear me.

And that is all I require.

"I was injured," I say, "while in pursuit of two of our defecting soldiers. Private Adam Kent and Private Kenji Kishimoto collaborated their escape in an effort to abduct Juliette Ferrars, our newest transfer and critical asset to Sector 45. They have been charged with the crime of unlawfully seizing and detaining Ms. Ferrars against her will. But, and most importantly, they have been rightly convicted of treason against The Reestablishment. When found, they will be executed on sight."

Terror, I realize, is one of the easiest feelings to read. Even on a soldier's stoic face.

"Second," I say, more slowly this time, "in an effort to expedite the process of stabilizing Sector 45, its citizens, and the ensuing chaos resulting from these recent disruptions, the supreme commander of The Reestablishment has joined us on base. He arrived," I tell them, "not thirty-six hours ago."

Some men have dropped their fists. Forgotten themselves. Their eyes are wide.

Petrified.

"You will welcome him," I say.

They drop to their knees.

It's strange, wielding this kind of power. I wonder if my father is proud of what he's created. That I'm able to bring thousands of grown men to their knees with only a few words; with only the sound of his title. It's a horrifying, addicting kind of thing.

I count five beats in my head.

"Rise."

They do. And then they march.

Five steps backward, forward, standing in place. They raise their left arms, curl their fingers into fists, and fall on one knee. This time, I do not let them up.

"Prepare yourselves, gentlemen," I say to them. "We will not rest until Kent and Kishimoto are found and Ms. Ferrars has returned to base. I will confer with the supreme commander in these next twenty-four hours; our newest mission will soon be clearly defined. In the interim you are to understand two things: first, that we will defuse the tension among the citizens and take pains to remind them of their promises to our new world. And second, be certain that we will find Privates Kent and Kishimoto." I stop. Look around, focusing on their faces. "Let their fates serve as an example to you. We do not welcome traitors in The Reestablishment. And we do not forgive."

TWELVE

One of my father's men is waiting for me outside my door.

I glance in his direction, but not long enough to discern his features. "State your business, soldier."

"Sir," he says, "I've been instructed to inform you that the supreme commander requests your presence in his quarters for dinner at twenty-hundred hours."

"Consider your message received." I move to unlock my door.

He steps forward, blocking my path.

I turn to face him.

He's standing less than a foot away from me: an implicit act of disrespect; a level of comfort even Delalieu does not allow himself. But unlike my men, the sycophants who surround my father consider themselves lucky. Being a member of the supreme commander's elite guard is considered a privilege and an honor. They answer to no one but him.

And right now, this soldier is trying to prove he outranks me.

He's jealous of me. He thinks I'm unworthy of being the son of the supreme commander of The Reestablishment. It's practically written on his face.

I have to stifle my impulse to laugh as I take in his cold gray eyes and the black pit that is his soul. He wears his sleeves rolled up above his elbows, his military tattoos clearly defined and on display. The concentric black bands of ink around his forearms are accented in red, green, and blue, the only sign on his person to indicate that he is a soldier highly elevated in rank. It's a sick branding ritual I've always refused to be a part of.

The soldier is still staring at me.

I incline my head in his direction, raise my eyebrows.

"I am required," he says, "to wait for verbal acceptance of this invitation."

I take a moment to consider my choices, which are none.

I, like the rest of the puppets in this world, am entirely subservient to my father's will. It's a truth I'm forced to contend with every day: that I've never been able to stand up to the man who has his fist clenched around my spine.

It makes me hate myself.

I meet the soldier's eyes again and wonder, for a fleeting moment, if he has a name, before I realize I couldn't possibly care less. "Consider it accepted."

"Yes, s—"

"And next time, soldier, you will not step within five feet of me without first asking permission."

He blinks, stunned. "Sir, I—"

"You are confused." I cut him off. "You assume your work with the supreme commander grants you immunity from rules that govern the lives of other soldiers. Here, you are mistaken."

His jaw tenses.

"Never forget," I say, quietly now, "that if I wanted your job, I could have it. And never forget that the man you so eagerly serve is the same man who taught me how to fire a gun when I was nine years old."

His nostrils flare. He stares straight ahead.

"Deliver your message, soldier. And then memorize this one: do not ever speak to me again."

His eyes are focused on a point directly behind me now, his shoulders rigid.

I wait.

His jaw is still tight. He slowly lifts his hand in salute.

"You are dismissed," I say.

I lock my bedroom door behind me and lean against it. I need just a moment. I reach for the bottle I left on my night-stand and shake out two of the square pills; I toss them into my mouth, closing my eyes as they dissolve. The darkness behind my eyelids is a welcome relief.

Until the memory of her face forces itself into my con-sciousness.

I sit down on my bed and drop my head into my hand. I shouldn't be thinking about her right now. I have hours of paperwork to sort through and the additional stress of my father's presence to contend with. Dinner with him should be a spectacle. A soul-crushing spectacle.

I squeeze my eyes shut tighter and make a weak effort to build the walls that would surely clear my mind. But this time, they don't work. Her face keeps cropping up, her journal taunting me from its place in my pocket. And I begin to realize that some small part of me doesn't want to wish away the thoughts of her. Some part of me enjoys the torture.

This girl is destroying me.

A girl who has spent the last year in an insane asylum. A girl who would try to shoot me dead for kissing her. A girl who ran off with another man just to get away from me.

Of course this is the girl I would fall for.

I close a hand over my mouth.

I am losing my mind.

I tug off my boots. Pull myself up onto my bed and allow my head to hit the pillows behind me.

She slept here, I think. She slept in my bed. She woke up in my bed. She was here and I let her get away.

I failed.

I lost her.

I don't even realize I've tugged her notebook out of my pocket until I'm holding it in front of my face. Staring at it. Studying the faded cover in an attempt to understand where she might've acquired such a thing. She must've stolen it from somewhere, though I can't imagine where.

There are so many things I want to ask her. So many things I wish I could say to her.

Instead, I open her journal, and read.

Sometimes I close my eyes and paint these walls a different color.

I imagine I'm wearing warm socks and sitting by a fire. I imagine someone's given me a book to read, a story to take me away from the torture of my own mind. I want to be someone else somewhere else with something else to fill my mind. I want to run, to feel the wind tug at my hair. I want to pretend that this is just a story within a story. That this cell is just a scene, that these hands don't belong to me, that this window leads to somewhere beautiful if only I could break it. I pretend this pillow is clean, I pretend this bed is soft. I pretend and pretend and pretend until the world becomes so breathtaking behind my eyelids that I can no longer contain it. But then my eyes fly open and I'm caught around the throat by a pair of hands that won't stop suffocating suffocating suffocating

My thoughts, I think, will soon be sound.

My mind, I hope, will soon be found.

The journal drops out of my hand and onto my chest. I run my only free hand across my face, through my hair. I rub the back of my neck and haul myself up so fast that my head hits the headboard and I'm actually grateful. I take a moment to appreciate the pain.

And then I pick up the book.

And turn the page.

I wonder what they're thinking. My parents. I wonder where they are. I wonder if they're okay now, if they're happy now, ~~if they finally got what they wanted~~. I wonder if my mother will ever have another child. I wonder if someone will ever be kind enough to kill me, and I wonder if hell is better than here. I wonder what my face looks like now. I wonder if I'll ever breathe fresh air again.

I wonder about so many things.

Sometimes I'll stay awake for days just counting everything I can find. I count the walls, the cracks in the walls, my fingers and toes. I count the springs in the bed, the threads in the blanket, the steps it takes to cross the room and back. I count my teeth and the individual hairs on my head and the number of seconds I can hold my breath.

But sometimes I get so tired that I forget I'm not allowed to wish for things anymore, and I find myself wishing for the one thing I've always wanted. The only thing I've always dreamt about.

I wish all the time for a friend.

I dream about it. I imagine what it would be like. To smile and be smiled upon. To have a person to confide in; someone who wouldn't throw things at me or stick my hands in the fire or beat me for being born. Someone who would hear that I'd been thrown away and would try to find me, who would never be afraid of me.

Someone who'd know I'd never try to hurt them.

I fold myself into a corner of this room and bury my head in my knees and rock back and forth and back and forth and back and forth and I wish and I wish and I wish and I dream of impossible things until I've cried myself to sleep.

I wonder what it would be like to have a friend.

And then I wonder who else is locked in this asylum. I wonder where the other screams are coming from.

I wonder if they're coming from me.

I'm trying to focus, telling myself these are just empty words, but I'm lying. Because somehow, just reading these words is too much; and the thought of her in pain is causing me an unbearable amount of agony.

To know that she experienced this.

She was thrown into this by her own parents, cast off and abused her entire life. Empathy is not an emotion I've ever known, but now it's drowning me, pulling me into a world I never knew I could enter. And though I've always believed she and I shared many things in common, I did not know how deeply I could feel it.

It's killing me.

I stand up. Start pacing the length of my bedroom until I've finally worked up the nerve to keep reading. Then I take a deep breath.

And turn the page.

~~There's something simmering inside of me.~~

~~Something I've never dared to tap into, something I'm afraid to acknowledge. There's a part of me clawing to break free from the cage I've trapped it in, banging on the doors of my heart, begging to be free.~~

~~Begging to let go.~~

~~Every day I feel like I'm reliving the same nightmare. I open my mouth to shout, to fight, to swing my fists, but my vocal cords are cut, my arms are heavy and weighted down as if trapped in wet cement and I'm screaming but no one can hear me, no one can reach me and I'm caught. And it's killing me.~~

~~I've always had to make myself submissive, subservient, twisted into a pleading, passive mop just to make everyone else feel safe and comfortable. My existence has become a fight to prove I'm harmless, that I'm not a threat, that I'm capable of living among other human beings without hurting them.~~

~~And I'm so tired I'm so tired I'm so tired I'm so tired and sometimes I get so angry.~~

I don't know what's happening to me.

"God, Juliette," I gasp.

And fall to my knees.

"Call for transport immediately." I need to get out. I need to get out right now.

"Sir? I mean, yes, sir, of course—but where—"

"I have to visit the compounds," I say. "I should make my rounds before my meeting this evening." This is both true and false. But I'm willing to do anything right now that might get my mind off this journal.

"Oh, certainly, sir. Would you like me to accompany you?"

"That won't be necessary, Lieutenant, but thank you for the offer."

"I—s-sir," he stammers. "Of course, it's m-my pleasure, sir, to assist you—"

Good God, I have taken leave of my senses. I never thank Delalieu. I've likely given the poor man a heart attack.

"I will be ready to go in ten minutes." I cut him off.

He stutters to a stop. Then, "Yes, sir. Thank you, sir."

I'm pressing my fist to my mouth as the call disconnects.

THIRTEEN

We had homes. Before.

All different kinds.

1-story homes. 2-story homes. 3-story homes.

We bought lawn ornaments and twinkle lights, learned to ride bikes without training wheels. We purchased lives confined within 1, 2, 3 stories already built, stories caught inside of structures we could not change.

We lived in those stories for a while.

We followed the tale laid out for us, the prose pinned down in every square foot of space we'd acquired. We were content with the plot twists that only mildly redirected our lives. We signed on the dotted line for the things we didn't know we cared about. We ate the things we shouldn't, spent money when we couldn't, lost sight of the Earth we had to inhabit and wasted wasted wasted everything. Food. Water. Resources.

Soon the skies were gray with chemical pollution, and the plants and animals were sick from genetic modification, and diseases rooted themselves in our air, our meals, our blood and bones. The food disappeared. The people were dying. Our empire fell to pieces.

The Reestablishment said they would help us. Save us.

Rebuild our society.

Instead they tore us all apart.

I enjoy coming to the compounds.

It's an odd place to seek refuge, but there's something about seeing so many civilians in such a vast, open space that reminds me of what I'm meant to be doing. I'm so often confined within the walls of Sector 45 headquarters that I forget the faces of those we're fighting and those we're fighting for.

I like to remember.

Most days I visit each cluster on the compounds; I greet the residents and ask about their living conditions. I can't help but be curious about what life must be like for them now. Because while the world changed for everyone else, it always stayed the same for me. Regimented. Isolated. Bleak.

There was a time when things were better, when my father wasn't always so angry. I was about four years old then. He used to let me sit on his lap and search his pockets. I'd get to keep anything I wanted as long as my argument was convincing enough. It was his idea of a game.

But this was all before.

I wrap my coat more tightly around my body, feel the material press against my back. I flinch without meaning to.

The life I know now is the only one that matters. The suffocation, the luxury, the sleepless nights, and the dead bodies. I've always been taught to focus on power and pain, gaining and inflicting.

I grieve nothing.

I take everything.

It's the only way I know how to live in this battered body. I empty my mind of the things that plague me and burden my soul, and I take all that I can from what little pleasantness comes my way. I do not know what it is to live a normal life; I do not know how to sympathize with the civilians who've lost their homes. I do not know what it must've been like for them before The Reestablishment took over.

So I enjoy touring the compounds.

I enjoy seeing how other people live; I like that the law requires them to answer my questions. I would have no way of knowing, otherwise.

But my timing is off.

I paid little attention to the clock before I left base and didn't realize how soon the sun would be setting. Most civilians are returning home to retire for the evening, their bodies bowed, huddled against the cold as they shuffle toward the metal clusters they share with at least three other families.

These makeshift homes are built from forty-foot shipping containers; they're stacked side by side and on top of one another, lumped together in groups of four and six. Each container has been insulated; fitted with two windows and one door. Stairs to the upper levels are attached on either side. The roofs are lined with solar panels that provide free electricity for each grouping.

It's something I'm proud of.

Because it was my idea.

When we were seeking temporary shelter for the civilians, I suggested refurbishing the old shipping containers that line the docks of every port around the world. Not only are they cheap, easily replicated, and highly customizable, but they're stackable, portable, and built to withstand the elements. They'd require minimal construction, and with the right team, thousands of housing units could be ready in a matter of days.

I'd pitched the idea to my father, thinking it might be the most effective option; a temporary solution that would be far less cruel than tents; something that would provide true, reliable shelter. But the result was so effective that The Reestablishment saw no need to upgrade. Here, on land that used to be a landfill, we've stacked thousands of containers; clusters of faded, rectangular cubes that are easy to monitor and keep track of.

The people are still told that these homes are temporary. That one day they will return to the memories of their old lives, and that things will be bright and beautiful again. But this is all a lie.

The Reestablishment has no plans to move them.

Civilians are caged on these regulated grounds; these containers have become their prisons. Everything has been numbered. The people, their homes, their level of importance to The Reestablishment.

Here, they've become a part of a huge experiment. A world wherein they work to support the needs of a regime that makes them promises it will never fulfill.

This is my life.

This sorry world.

Most days I feel just as caged as these civilians; and that's likely why I always come here. It's like running from one prison to another; an existence wherein there is no relief, no refuge. Where even my own mind is a traitor.

I should be stronger than this.

I've been training for just over a decade. Every day I've worked to hone my physical and mental strengths. I'm five feet, nine inches and 170 pounds of muscle. I've been built to survive, to maximize endurance and stamina, and I'm most comfortable when I'm holding a gun in my hand. I can fieldstrip, clean, reload, disassemble, and reassemble more than 150 different types of firearms. I can shoot a target through the center from almost any distance. I can break a person's windpipe with only the edge of my hand. I can temporarily paralyze a man with nothing but my knuckles.

On the battlefield, I'm able to disconnect myself from the motions I've been taught to memorize. I've developed a reputation as a cold, unfeeling monster who fears nothing and cares for less.

But this is all very deceiving.

Because the truth is, I am nothing but a coward.

FOURTEEN

The sun is setting.

Soon I'll have no choice but to return to base, where I'll have to sit still and listen to my father speak instead of shooting a bullet through his open mouth.

So I stall for time.

I watch from afar as the children run around while their parents herd them home. I wonder about how one day they'll get old enough to realize that the Reestablishment Registration cards they carry are actually tracking their every movement. That the money their parents make from working in whichever factories they were sorted into is closely monitored. These children will grow up and finally understand that everything they do is recorded, every conversation dissected for whispers of rebellion. They don't know that profiles are created for every citizen, and that every profile is thick with documentation on their friendships, relationships, and work habits; even the ways in which they choose to spend their free time.

We know everything about everyone.

Too much.

So much, in fact, that I seldom remember we're dealing with real, live people until I see them on the compounds.

I've memorized the names of nearly every person in Sector 45. I like to know who lives within my jurisdiction, soldiers and civilians alike.

That's how I knew, for example, that Private Seamus Fletcher, 45B-76423, was beating his wife and children every night.

I knew he was spending all his money on alcohol; I knew he'd been starving his family. I monitored the REST dollars he spent at our supply centers and carefully observed his family on the compounds. I knew his three children were all under the age of ten and hadn't eaten in weeks; I knew that they'd repeatedly been to the compounds' medic for broken bones and stitches. I knew he'd punched his nine-year-old daughter in the mouth and split her lip, fractured her jaw, and broken her two front teeth; and I knew his wife was pregnant. I also knew that he hit her so hard one night she lost the child the following morning.

I knew, because I was there.

I'd been stopping by each residence, visiting with the civilians, asking questions about their health and overall living situations. I'd wanted to know about their work conditions and whether any members of their family were ill and needed to be quarantined.

She was there that day. Fletcher's wife. Her nose was broken so badly that both her eyes had swollen shut. Her frame was so thin and frail, her color so sallow that I thought she might snap in half just by sitting down. But when I asked about her injuries, she wouldn't look me in the eye. She said she'd fallen down; that because of her fall, she'd lost the pregnancy and managed to break her nose in the process.

I nodded. Thanked her for her cooperation in answering my questions.

And then I called for an assembly.

I'm well aware that the majority of my soldiers steal from our storage compounds. I oversee our inventory closely, and I know that supplies go missing all the time. But I allow these infractions because they do not upset the system. A few extra loaves of bread or bars of soap keep my soldiers in better spirits; they work harder if they are healthy, and most are supporting spouses, children, and relatives. So it is a concession I allow.

But there are some things I do not forgive.

I don't consider myself a moral man. I do not philosophize about life or bother with the laws and principles that govern most people. I do not pretend to know the difference between right and wrong. But I do live by a certain kind of code. And sometimes, I think, you have to learn how to shoot first.

Seamus Fletcher was murdering his family. And I shot him in the forehead because I thought it'd be kinder than ripping him to pieces by hand.

But my father picked up where Fletcher left off. My father had three children and their mother shot dead, all because of the drunken bastard they'd depended on to provide for them. He was their father, her husband, and the reason they all died a brutal, untimely death.

And some days I wonder why I insist on keeping myself alive.

FIFTEEN

Once I'm back on base, I head straight down.

I ignore the soldiers and their salutes as I pass by, paying little attention to the blend of curiosity and suspicion in their eyes. I didn't even realize I was headed this way until I arrived at headquarters; but my body seems to know more about what I need right now than my mind does. My footfalls are heavy; the steady, clipping sound of my boots echoes along the stone path as I reach the lower levels.

I haven't been here in nearly two weeks.

The room has been rebuilt since my last visit; the glass panel and the concrete wall have been replaced. And as far as I'm aware, she was the last person to use this room.

I brought her here myself.

I push through a set of swinging double doors into the locker room that sits adjacent to the simulation deck. My hand searches for a switch in the dark; the light beeps once before it flickers to life. A dull hum of electricity vibrates through these vast dimensions. Everything is quiet, abandoned.

Just as I like it.

I strip as quickly as this injured arm will allow me to. I still have two hours before I'm expected to meet my father for dinner, so I shouldn't be feeling so anxious, but my nerves are not cooperating. Everything seems to be catching up with me at once. My failures. My cowardice. My stupidity.

Sometimes I'm just so tired of this life.

I'm standing barefoot on this concrete floor in nothing but an arm sling, hating the way this injury constantly slows me down. I grab the shorts stashed in my locker and pull them on as quickly as I can, leaning against the wall for support. When I'm finally upright, I slam the locker shut and make my way into the adjoining room.

I hit another switch, and the main operational deck whirs to life. The computers beep and flash as the program recalibrates; I run my fingers along the keyboard.

We use these rooms to generate simulations.

We manipulate the technology to create environments and experiences that exist entirely in the human mind. Not only are we able to create the framework, but we can also control minute details. Sounds, smells, false confidence, paranoia. The program was originally designed to help train soldiers for specific missions, as well as aid them in overcoming fears that would otherwise cripple them on the battlefield.

I use it for my own purposes.

I used to come here all the time before she arrived on base. This was my safe space; my only escape from the world. I only wish it didn't come with a uniform. These shorts are starchy and uncomfortable, the polyester itchy and irritating.

But the shorts are lined with a special chemical that reacts with my skin and feeds information to the sensors; it helps place me in the experience, and will enable to me to run for miles without ever running into actual, physical walls in my true environment. And in order for the process to be as effective as possible, I have to be wearing next to nothing. The cameras are hypersensitive to body heat, and work best when not in contact with synthetic materials.

I'm hoping this detail will be fixed in the next generation of the program.

The mainframe prompts me for information; I quickly enter an access code that grants me clearance to pull up a history of my past simulations. I look up and over my shoulder as the computer processes the data; I glance through the newly repaired two-way mirror that sees into the main chamber. I still can't believe she broke down an entire wall of glass and concrete and managed to walk away uninjured.

Incredible.

The machine beeps twice; I spin back around. The programs in my history are loaded and ready to be executed.

Her file is at the top of the list.

I take a deep breath; try to shake off the memory. I don't regret putting her through such a horrifying experience; I don't know that she would've ever allowed herself to finally lose control—to finally inhabit her own body—if I hadn't found an effective method of provoking her. Ultimately, I really believe it helped her, just as I intended it to. But I do wish she hadn't pointed a gun at my face and jumped out a window shortly afterward.

I take another slow, steadying breath.

And select the simulation I came here for.

SIXTEEN

I'm standing in the main chamber.

Facing myself.

This is a very simple simulation. I didn't change my clothes or my hair or even the room's carpeted floors. I didn't do anything at all except create a duplicate of myself and hand him a gun.

He won't stop staring at me.

One.

He cocks his head. "Are you ready?" A pause. "Are you scared?"

My heart kicks into gear.

He lifts his arm. Smiles a little. "Don't worry," he says. "It's almost over now."

Two.

"Just a little longer and I'll leave," he says, pointing the gun directly at my forehead.

My palms are sweating. My pulse is racing.

"You'll be all right," he lies. "I promise."

Three.

Boom.

SEVENTEEN

"You sure you're not hungry?" my father asks, still chewing. "This is really quite good."

I shift in my seat. Focus on the ironed creases in these pants I'm wearing.

"Hm?" he asks. I can actually hear him smiling.

I'm acutely aware of the soldiers lining the walls of this room. He always keeps them close, and always in constant competition with one another. Their first assignment was to determine which of the eleven of them was the weakest link. The one with the most convincing argument was then required to dispose of his target.

My father finds these practices amusing.

"I'm afraid I'm not hungry. The medicine," I lie, "destroys my appetite."

"Ah," he says. I hear him put his utensils down. "Of course. How inconvenient."

I say nothing.

"Leave us."

Two words and his men disperse in a matter of seconds. The door slides shut behind them.

"Look at me," he says.

I look up, my eyes carefully devoid of emotion. I hate his

face. I can't stand to look at him for too long; I don't like experiencing the full impact of how very inhuman he is. He is not tortured by what he does or how he lives. In fact, he enjoys it. He loves the rush of power; he thinks of himself as an invincible entity.

And in some ways, he's not wrong.

I've come to believe that the most dangerous man in the world is the one who feels no remorse. The one who never apologizes and therefore seeks no forgiveness. Because in the end it is our emotions that make us weak, not our actions.

I turn away.

"What did you find?" he asks, with no preamble.

My mind immediately goes to the journal I've stowed away in my pocket, but I make no movement. I do not dare flinch. People seldom realize that they tell lies with their lips and truths with their eyes all the time. Put a man in a room with something he's hidden and then ask him where he's hidden it; he'll tell you he doesn't know; he'll tell you you've got the wrong man; but he'll almost always glance at its exact location. And right now I know my father is watching me, waiting to see where I might look, what I might say next.

I keep my shoulders relaxed and take a slow, imperceptible breath to steady my heart. I do not respond. I pretend to be lost in thought.

"Son?"

I look up. Feign surprise. "Yes?"

"What did you find? When you searched her room today?"

I exhale. Shake my head as I lean back in my chair. "Broken glass. A disheveled bed. Her armoire, hanging open. She took only a few toiletries and some extra pairs of clothes and undergarments. Nothing else was out of place." None of this is a lie.

I hear him sigh. He pushes away his plate.

I feel the outline of her notebook burning against my upper leg.

"And you say you do not know where she might've gone?"

"I only know that she, Kent, and Kishimoto must be together," I tell him. "Delalieu says they stole a car, but the trace disappeared abruptly at the edge of a barren field. We've had troops on patrol for days now, searching the area, but they've found nothing."

"And where," he says, "do you plan on searching next? Do you think they might've crossed over into another sector?" His voice is off. Entertained.

I glance up at his smiling face.

He's only asking me these questions to test me. He has his own answers, his own solution already prepared. He wants to watch me fail by answering incorrectly. He's trying to prove that without him, I'd make all the wrong decisions.

He's mocking me.

"No," I tell him, my voice solid, steady. "I don't think they'd do something as idiotic as cross into another sector. They don't have the access, the means, or the capacity. Both men were severely wounded, rapidly losing blood, and too far from any source of emergency aid. They're probably dead by now. The girl is likely the only survivor, and she can't have gone far because she has no idea how to navigate these areas. She's been blind to them for too long; everything in this environment is foreign to her. Furthermore, she does not know how to drive, and if she'd somehow managed to commandeer a vehicle, we would've received word of stolen property. Considering her overall health, her propensity toward physical inexertion, and her general lack of access to food, water, and medical attention, she's probably collapsed within a five-mile radius of this supposed barren field. We have to find her before she freezes to death."

My father clears his throat.

"Yes," he says, "those are interesting theories. And perhaps under ordinary circumstances, they might actually hold true. But you are failing to recall the most important detail."

I meet his gaze.

"She is not normal," he says, leaning back in his chair. "And she is not the only one of her kind."

My heartbeat quickens. I blink too fast.

"Oh come now, surely you'd suspected? You'd hypothesized?" He laughs. "It seems statistically impossible that she'd be the only mistake manufactured by our world. You knew this, but you didn't want to believe it. And I came here to tell you that it's true." He cocks his head at me. Smiles a big, vibrant smile. "There are more of them. And they've recruited her."

"No," I breathe.

"They infiltrated your troops. Lived among you in secret. And now they've stolen your toy and run away with it. God only knows how they hope to manipulate her for their own benefit."

"How can you be certain?" I ask. "How do you know they've succeeded in taking her with them? Kent was half-dead when I left him—"

"Pay attention, son. I'm telling you that they are not normal. They do not follow your rules; there is no logic that binds them. You have no idea what oddities they might be capable of." A pause. "Furthermore, I have known for some time now that a group of them exists undercover in this area. But in all these years they've always kept to themselves. They did not interfere with my methods, and I thought it best to allow them to die off on their own without infecting in our civilians unnecessary panic. You understand, of course," he says. "After all, you could hardly contain even one of them. They're freakish things to behold."

"You knew?" I'm on my feet now. Trying to stay calm. "You knew of their existence, all this time, and yet you did nothing? You said nothing?"

"It seemed unnecessary."

"And now?" I demand.

"Now it seems pertinent."

"Unbelievable!" I throw my hands in the air. "That you would withhold such information from me! When you knew of my plans for her—when you knew what pains I'd taken to bring her here—"

"Calm yourself," he says. He stretches out his legs; rests the ankle of one on the knee of the other. "We are going to find them. This barren field Delalieu speaks of—the area where the car was no longer traceable? That is our target location. They must be located underground. We must find the entrance and destroy them quietly, from within. Then we will have punished the guilty among them, and kept the rest from rising up and inspiring rebellion in our people."

He leans forward.

"The civilians hear everything. And right now they are vibrating with a new kind of energy. They're feeling inspired that anyone was able to run away, and that you've been wounded in the process. It makes our defenses seem weak and easily penetrable. We must destroy this perception by righting the imbalance. Fear will return everything to its proper place."

"But they've been searching," I tell him. "My men. Every day they've scoured the area and found nothing. How can we be sure we'll find anything at all?"

"Because," he says, "you will lead them. Every night. After curfew, while the civilians are asleep. You will cease your daylight searches; you will not give the citizens any-thing else to talk about. Act quietly, son. Do not show your moves. I will remain on base and oversee your responsibilities through my men; I will dictate to Delalieu as necessary. And in the interim, you shall find them, so that I may destroy them as swiftly as possible. This nonsense has gone on long enough," he says, "and I'm no longer feeling gracious."

EIGHTEEN

I'm sorry. I'm so sorry. I'm so sorry I'm so sorry I'm so so sorry I'm so sorry. I'm so sorry I'm so sorry I'm so so sorry. I'm so sorry. I'm so sorry. I'm so sorry I'm so so sorry I'm so sorry I'm so sorry I'm so sorry I'm so so sorry. I'm so sorry. I'm so sorry I'm so sorry I'm so so sorry I'm so sorry. I'm so sorry. I'm so sorry I'm so so sorry. I'm so sorry. I'm so sorry I'm so sorry I'm so so sorry I'm so sorry. I'm so sorry I'm so sorry. I'm so so sorry. I'm so sorry. I'm so sorry I'm so sorry I'm so so sorry I'm so sorry. I'm so sorry. I'm so sorry I'm so so sorry. I'm sorry I'm so sorry please forgive me.

 It was an accident.

 Forgive me

 Please forgive me

There is little I allow anyone to discover about me. There's even less I'm willing to share about myself. And of the many things I've never discussed, this is one of them.

I like to take long baths.

I've had an obsession with cleanliness for as long as I can remember. I've always been so mired in death and destruction that I think I've overcompensated by keeping myself pristine as much as possible. I take frequent showers. I brush and floss three times a day. I trim my own hair every week. I scrub my hands and nails before I go to bed and just after I wake up. I have an unhealthy preoccupation with wearing only freshly laundered clothes. And whenever I'm experiencing any extreme level of emotion, the only thing that settles my nerves is a long bath.

So that's what I'm doing right now.

The medics taught me how to bind my injured arm in the same plastic they used before, so I'm able to sink beneath the surface without a problem. I submerge my head for a long while, holding my breath as I exhale through my nose. I feel the small bubbles rise to the surface.

The warm water makes me feel weightless. It carries my burdens for me, understanding that I need a moment to relieve my shoulders of this weight. To close my eyes and relax.

My face breaks the surface.

I don't open my eyes; only my nose and lips meet the oxygen on the other side. I take small, even breaths to help steady my mind. It's so late that I don't know what time it is; all I know is that the temperature has dropped significantly, and the cold air is tickling my nose. It's a strange sensation, to have 98 percent of my body floating at a warm, welcome temperature, while my nose and lips twitch from the cold.

I sink my face below the water again.

I could live here, I think. Live where gravity does not know my name. Here I am unbound, untethered by the chains of this life. I am a different body, a different shell, and my weight is carried by the hands of friends. So many nights I've wished I could fall asleep under this sheet.

I sink deeper.

In one week my entire life has changed.

My priorities, shifted. My concentration, destroyed. Everything I care about right now revolves around one person, and for the first time in my life, it's not myself. Her words have been burned into my mind. I can't stop picturing her as she must've been, can't stop imagining what she must've experienced. Finding her journal has crippled me. My feelings for her have spiraled out of control. I've never been so desperate to see her, to talk to her.

I want her to know that I understand now. That I didn't understand before. She and I really are the same; in so many more ways than I could've known.

But now she's out of reach. She's gone somewhere with strangers who do not know her and would not care for her as I would. She's been dropped into another foreign environment with no time to transition, and I'm worried about her. A person in her situation—with her past—does not recover overnight. And now, one of two things is bound to happen: She's either going to completely shut down, or she's going to explode.

I sit up too fast, breaking free of the water, gasping for air.

I push my wet hair out of my face. I lean back against the tiled wall, allowing the cool air to calm me, to clear my thoughts.

I have to find her before she breaks.

I've never wanted to cooperate with my father before, never wanted to agree with his motives or his methods. But in this instance, I'm willing to do just about anything to get her back.

And I'm eager for any opportunity to snap Kent's neck.

That traitorous bastard. The idiot who thinks he's won himself a pretty girl. He has no idea who she is. No idea what she's about to become.

And if he thinks he's even remotely suited to match her, he's even more of an idiot than I gave him credit for.

NINETEEN

"Where's the coffee?" I ask, my eyes scanning the table.

Delalieu drops his fork. The silverware clangs against the china plates. He looks up, eyes wide. "Sir?"

"I'd like to try it," I tell him, attempting to spread butter on my toast with my left hand. I toss a look in his direction. "You're always going on about your coffee, aren't you? I thought I—"

Delalieu jumps up from the table without a word. Bolts out the door.

I laugh silently into my plate.

Delalieu carts the tea and coffee tray in himself and stations it by my chair. His hands shake as he pours the dark liquid into a teacup, places it on a saucer, sets it on the table, and pushes it in my direction.

I wait until he's finally sitting down again before I take a sip. It's a strange, obscenely bitter sort of drink; not at all what I expected. I glance up at him, surprised to discover that a man like Delalieu would begin his day by bracing himself with such a potent, foul-tasting liquid. I find I respect him for it.

"This isn't terrible," I tell him.

His face splits into a smile so wide, so beatific, I wonder if he's misheard me. He's practically beaming when he says, "I take mine with cream and sugar. The taste is far better that w—"

"Sugar." I put my cup down. Press my lips together, fight back a smile. "You add sugar to it. Of course you do. That makes so much more sense."

"Would you like some, sir?"

I hold up my hand. Shake my head. "Call back the troops, Lieutenant. We're going to halt daytime missions and instead launch in the evening, after curfew. You will remain on base," I tell him, "where the supreme will dictate orders through his men; carry out any demands as they are required. I shall lead the group myself." I stop. Hold his eyes. "There will be no more talk of what has transpired. Nothing for the civilians to see or speak of. Do you understand?"

"Yes, sir," he says, his coffee forgotten. "I'll issue the orders at once."

"Good."

He stands up.

I nod.

He leaves.

I'm beginning to feel real hope for the first time since she left. We're going to find her. Now, with this new information—with an entire army against a group of clueless rebels—it seems impossible we won't.

I take a deep breath. Take another sip of this coffee.

I'm surprised to discover how much I enjoy the bitter taste of it.

TWENTY

He's waiting for me when I return to my room.

"The orders have been issued," I tell him without looking in his direction. "We will mobilize tonight." I hesitate. "So if you'll excuse me, I have other matters to contend with."

"What's it like," he asks, "to be so crippled?" He's smiling. "How can you stand to look at yourself, knowing that you've been disabled by your own subordinates?"

I pause outside the adjoining door to my office. "What do you want?"

"What," he says, "is your fascination with that girl?"

My spine goes rigid.

"She is more to you than just an experiment, isn't she?" he says.

I turn around slowly. He's standing in the middle of my room, hands in his pockets, smiling at me like he might be disgusted.

"What are you talking about?"

"Look at yourself," he says. "I haven't even said her name and you fall apart." He shakes his head, still studying me. "Your face is pale, your only working hand is clenched.

You're breathing too fast, and your entire body is tense." A pause. "You have betrayed yourself, son. You think you're very clever," he says, "but you're forgetting who taught you your tricks."

I go hot and cold all at once. I try to unclench my fist and I can't. I want to tell him he's wrong, but I'm suddenly feeling unsteady, wishing I'd eaten more at breakfast, and then wishing I'd eaten nothing at all.

"I have work to do," I manage to say.

"Tell me," he says, "that you would not care if she died along with the others."

"What?" The nervous, shaky word escapes my lips too soon.

My father drops his eyes. Clasps and unclasps his hands. "You have disappointed me in so many ways," he says, his voice deceptively soft. "Please don't let this be another."

For a moment I feel as though I exist outside of my body, as if I'm looking at myself from his perspective. I see my face, my injured arm, these legs that suddenly seem unable to carry my weight. Cracks begin to form along my face, all the way down my arms, my torso, my legs.

I imagine this is what it's like to fall apart.

I don't realize he's said my name until he repeats it twice more.

"What do you want from me?" I ask, surprised to hear how calm I sound. "You've walked into my room without permission; you stand here and accuse me of things I don't have time to understand. I am following your rules, your orders. We will leave tonight; we will find their hideout. You can destroy them as you see fit."

"And your girl," he says, cocking his head at me. "Your Juliette?"

I flinch at the sound of her name. My pulse is racing so fast it feels like a whisper.

"If I were to shoot three holes in her head, how would that make you feel?" He stares at me. Watches me. "Disappointed, because you'd have lost your pet project? Or devastated, because you'd have lost the girl you love?"

Time seems to slow down, melting all around me.

"It would be a waste," I say, ignoring the tremble I feel deep inside me, threatening to tip me over, "to lose something I've invested so much time in."

He smiles. "It's good to know you see it that way," he says. "But projects are, after all, easily replaced. And I'm certain we'll be able to find a better, more practical use of your time."

I blink at him so slowly. Part of my chest feels as if it's collapsed.

"Of course," I hear myself say.

"I knew you'd understand." He claps me on my injured shoulder as he leaves. My knees nearly buckle. "It was a good effort, son. But she's cost us too much time and expense, and she's proven completely useless. This way we'll be disposing of many inconveniences all at once. We'll just consider her collateral damage." He shoots me one last smile before walking past me and out the door.

I fall back against the wall.
    And crumble to the floor.

TWENTY-ONE

Swallow the tears back often enough and they'll start
feeling like acid dripping down your throat.

    It's that terrible moment when you're sitting still so
still so still because ~~you don't want them to see you cry~~ *you*
don't want to cry but your lips won't stop trembling and
your eyes are filled to the brim with please and I beg you
and please and I'm sorry and please and have mercy and
maybe this time it'll be different but it's always the same.
There's no one to run to for comfort. No one on your side.

    Light a candle for me, I used to whisper to no one.

    Someone

    Anyone

    If you're out there

    Please tell me you can feel this fire.

It's day five of our patrols, and still, nothing.

I lead the group every night, marching into the silence
of these cold, winter landscapes. We search for hidden pas-
sageways, camouflaged manholes—any indication that
there might be another world under our feet.

And every night we return to base with nothing.

The futility of these past few days has washed over me,

dulling my senses, settling me into a kind of daze I haven't been able to claw my way out of. Every day I wake up searching for a solution to the problems I've forced upon myself, but I have no idea how to fix this.

If she's out there, he will find her. And he will kill her.

Just to teach me a lesson.

My only hope is to find her first. Maybe I could hide her. Or tell her to run. Or pretend she's already dead. Or maybe I'll convince him that she's different, better than the others; that she's worth keeping alive.

I sound like a pathetic, desperate idiot.

I am a child all over again, hiding in dark corners and praying he won't find me. Hoping he'll be in a good mood today. That maybe everything will be all right. That maybe my mother won't be screaming this time.

How quickly I revert back to another version of myself in his presence.

I've gone numb.

I've been performing my tasks with a sort of mechanical dedication; it requires minimal effort. Moving is simple enough. Eating is something I've grown accustomed to.

I can't stop reading her notebook.

My heart actually hurts, somehow, but I can't stop turning the pages. I feel as if I'm pounding against an invisible wall, as if my face has been bandaged in plastic and I can't breathe, can't see, can't hear any sound but my own heart beating in my ears.

I've wanted few things in this life.

I've asked for nothing from no one.

And now, all I'm asking for is another chance. An opportunity to see her again. But unless I can find a way to stop him, these words will be all I'll ever have of her.

These paragraphs and sentences. These letters.

I've become obsessed. I carry her notebook with me everywhere I go, spending all my free moments trying to decipher the words she's scribbled in the margins, developing stories to go along with the numbers she's written down.

I've also noticed that the last page is missing. Ripped out.

I can't help but wonder why. I've searched through the book a hundred times, looking for other sections where pages might be gone, but I've found none. And somehow I feel cheated, knowing there's a piece I might've missed. It's not even my journal; it's none of my business at all, but I've read her words so many times now that they feel like my own. I can practically recite them from memory.

It's strange being in her head without being able to see her. I feel like she's here, right in front of me. I feel like I now know her so intimately, so privately. I'm safe in the company of her thoughts; I feel welcome, somehow. Understood. So much so that some days I manage to forget that she's the one who put this bullet hole in my arm.

I almost forget that she still hates me, despite how hard I've fallen for her.

And I've fallen.

So hard.

I've hit the ground. Gone right through it. Never in my life have I felt this. Nothing like this. I've felt shame and cowardice, weakness and strength. I've known terror and indifference, self-hate and general disgust. I've seen things that cannot be unseen.

And yet I've known nothing like this terrible, horrible, paralyzing feeling. I feel crippled. Desperate and out of control. And it keeps getting worse. Every day I feel sick. Empty and somehow aching.

Love is a heartless bastard.

I'm driving myself insane.

I fall backward onto my bed, fully dressed. Coat, boots, gloves. I'm too tired to take them off. These late-night shifts have left me very little time to sleep. I feel as though I've been existing in a constant state of exhaustion.

My head hits the pillow and I blink once. Twice.

I collapse.

TWENTY-TWO

"No," I hear myself say. "You're not supposed to be here."

She's sitting on my bed. She's leaning back on her elbows, legs outstretched in front of her, crossed at the ankles. And while some part of me understands I must be dreaming, there's another, overwhelmingly dominant part of me that refuses to accept this. Part of me wants to believe she's really here, inches away from me, wearing this short, tight black dress that keeps slipping up her thighs. But everything about her looks different, oddly vibrant; the colors are all wrong. Her lips are a richer, deeper shade of pink; her eyes seem wider, darker. She's wearing shoes I know she'd never wear. And strangest of all: she's smiling at me.

"Hi," she whispers.

It's just one word, but my heart is already racing. I'm inching away from her, stumbling back and nearly slamming my skull against the headboard, when I realize my shoulder is no longer wounded. I look down at myself. My arms are both fully functional. I'm wearing nothing but a white T-shirt and my underwear.

She shifts positions in an instant, propping herself up on her knees before crawling over to me. She climbs onto my lap. She's now straddling my waist. I'm suddenly breathing too fast.

Her lips are at my ear. Her words are so soft. "Kiss me," she says.

"Juliette—"

"I came all the way here." She's still smiling at me. It's a rare smile, the kind she's never honored me with. But somehow, right now, she's mine. She's mine and she's perfect and she wants me, and I'm not going to fight it.

I don't want to.

Her hands are tugging at my shirt, pulling it up over my head. Tossing it to the floor. She leans forward and kisses my neck, just once, so slowly. My eyes fall closed.

There aren't enough words in this world to describe what I'm feeling.

I feel her hands move down my chest, my stomach; her fingers run along the edge of my underwear. Her hair falls forward, grazing my skin, and I have to clench my fists to keep from pinning her to my bed.

Every nerve ending in my body is awake. I've never felt so alive or so desperate in my life, and I'm sure if she could hear what I'm thinking right now, she'd run out the door and never come back.

Because I want her.

Now.

Here.

Everywhere.

I want nothing between us.

I want her clothes off and the lights on and I want to study her. I want to unzip her out of this dress and take my time with every inch of her. I can't help my need to just stare; to know her and her features: the slope of her nose, the curve of her lips, the line of her jaw. I want to run my fingertips across the soft skin of her neck and trace it all the way down. I want to feel the weight of her pressed against me, wrapped around me.

I can't remember a reason why this can't be right or real. I can't focus on anything but the fact that she's sitting on my lap, touching my chest, staring into my eyes like she might really love me.

I wonder if I've actually died.

But just as I lean in, she leans back, grinning before reaching behind her, never once breaking eye contact with me. "Don't worry," she whispers. "It's almost over now."

Her words seem so strange, so familiar. "What do you mean?"

"Just a little longer and I'll leave."

"No." I'm blinking fast, reaching for her. "No, don't go—where are you going—"

"You'll be all right," she says. "I promise."

"*No*—"

But now she's holding a gun.

And pointing it at my heart.

TWENTY-THREE

These letters are all I have left.

26 friends to tell my stories to.

26 letters are all I need. I can stitch them together to create oceans and ecosystems. I can fit them together to form planets and solar systems. I can use letters to construct skyscrapers and metropolitan cities populated by people, places, things, and ideas that are more real to me than these 4 walls.

I need nothing but letters to live. Without them I would not exist.

Because these words I write down are the only proof I have that I'm still alive.

It's extraordinarily cold this morning.

I suggested we make a smaller, more low-key trip to the compounds earlier in the day today, just to see if any of the civilians seemed suspicious or out of place. I'm beginning to wonder if Kent and Kishimoto and all the others are living among the people in secret. They must, after all, have to have some source for food and water—something that ties them to society; I doubt they can grow anything underground. But of course, these are all assumptions. They might very well have a person who can grow food out of thin air.

I quickly address my men; instruct them to disperse and remain inconspicuous. Their job is to watch everyone today, and report their findings directly to me.

Once they're gone, I'm left to look around and be alone with my thoughts. It's a dangerous place to be.

God, she seemed so real in my dream.

I close my eyes, dragging a hand down my face; my fingers linger against my lips. I could feel her. I could really *feel* her. Even thinking about it now makes my heart race. I don't know what I'm going to do if I keep having such intense dreams about her. I won't be able to function at all.

I take a deep, steadying breath and focus. I allow my eyes to wander naturally, and I can't help but be distracted by the children running around. They seem so spirited and carefree. In a strange way, it makes me sad that they've been able to find happiness in this life. They have no idea what they've missed; no idea what the world used to be like.

Something barrels into the backs of my legs.

I hear a strange, labored sort of panting; I turn around.

It's a dog.

A tired, starving dog, so thin and frail it looks like it could be knocked over by the wind. But it's staring at me. Unafraid. Mouth open. Tongue lolling.

I want to laugh out loud.

I glance around quickly before scooping the dog into my arms. I don't need to give my father any more reasons to castrate me, and I don't trust my soldiers not to report something like this.

That I would play with a dog.

I can already hear the things my father would say to me.

I carry the whimpering creature over to one of the recently vacated housing units—I just saw all three families leave for work—and duck down behind one of the fences. The dog seems smart enough to understand that now is not the time to bark.

I tug off my glove and reach into my pocket for the Danish I grabbed at breakfast this morning; I hadn't had a chance to eat anything before our early start today. And though I haven't the faintest idea what dogs eat, exactly, I offer the Danish anyway.

The dog practically bites off my hand.

It chokes down the Danish in two bites and starts licking my fingers, jumping against my chest in excitement, finally plowing into the warmth of my open coat. I can't control the easy laughter that escapes my lips; I don't want to. I haven't felt like laughing in so long. And I can't help but be amazed at the power such small, unassuming animals wield over us; they so easily break down our defenses.

I run my hand along its shabby fur, feeling its ribs jut out at sharp, uncomfortable angles. But the dog doesn't seem to mind its starved state, at least not right now. Its tail is wagging hard, and it keeps pulling back from my coat to look me in the eye. I'm starting to wish I'd stuffed all the Danishes in my pocket this morning.

Something snaps.

I hear a gasp.

I spin around.

I jump up, alert, searching for the sound. It seemed close by. Someone saw me. Someone—

A civilian. She's already darting away, her body pressed against the wall of a nearby unit.

"Hey!" I shout. "You there—"

She stops. Looks up.

I nearly collapse.

Juliette.

She's staring at me. She's actually here, staring at me, her eyes wide and panicked. My legs are suddenly made of lead. I'm rooted to the ground, unable to form words. I don't even know where to start. There's so much I want to say to her, so much I've never told her, and I'm just so happy to see her—God, I'm so *relieved*—

She's disappeared.

I spin around, frantic, wondering whether I've actually begun to lose my grip on reality. My eyes land on the little dog still sitting there, waiting for me, and I stare at it, dumbfounded, wondering what on earth just happened. I keep looking back at the place I thought I saw her, but I see nothing.

Nothing.

I run a hand through my hair, so confused, so horrified and angry with myself that I'm tempted to rip it out of my head.

What is happening to me.

FRACTURE ME

ONE

"Addie? Addie, wake up. *Addie*—"

I roll over with a groan and stretch, rubbing both eyes with the heel of my hand. It's too early for this shit.

"Addie—"

Still half asleep, I grab James by the collar and yank him down, shoving his head under the blanket. He shouts and I laugh, wrapping him up in the sheets until he can't get out.

"Stooooop iiiiiiit," he whines, little fists pounding against the sheets. "Addie, let me out—"

"Hey—how many times have I told you to stop calling me that?"

James tries to punch me through the blanket. I pick him up and flip him over in my arms and he screams, his legs kicking wildly.

"You're so mean," he cries, wriggling around in my grip. "If Kenji were here, he would never let y—"

At that, I freeze, and James can feel it. He goes quiet in my arms, and I let him go. He untangles himself from my sheets, and we stare at each other.

James blinks. His bottom lip trembles and he bites down on it. "Do you know if he's okay?"

I shake my head.

Kenji is still in the medical wing. No one knows for sure what happened yet, but people have been talking. Whispering.

I look toward the wall. James is still speaking, but I'm too distracted to pay attention.

It's hard for me to believe Juliette could hurt anyone like that.

"Everyone says he's gone," James is saying now.

This, I catch.

"What?" I turn back, alarmed. "How?"

James shrugs. "I don't know. They said he broke out of his room."

"What are you talking about? How could he break out of his room—?"

James shrugs again. "I don't think he wanted to be here anymore."

"But—what?" I screw up my face, confused. "Does that mean he's feeling better? Did someone tell you he was feeling better?"

James frowns. "Did you want him to feel better? I thought you didn't like him."

I sigh. Run a hand through the back of my hair. "Of course I like him. I know we don't always get along, but it's really close quarters in here, and he's always got so many damn opinions—"

James shoots me a strange look. "So . . . you don't want to kill him? You're always saying you want to kill him."

"I'm not serious when I say stuff like that." I try not to

114

roll my eyes. "He and I have been friends for a long time. I'm actually worried about him."

"Okay," James says carefully. "You're weird, Addie."

I can't help but laugh a little. "Why am I weird? And hey, stop calling me Addie—you know how much I hate that—"

"Yeah, and I still don't know why." He cuts me off. "Mom always used to call you Addie—"

"Well Mom's dead, isn't she?" My voice has gone hard. My hands are clenched. And when I see the look on James's face, I'm instantly sorry for being so harsh. I release my fists. Take a deep breath.

James swallows hard. "Sorry," he says quietly.

I nod, look away. "Yeah. Me too." I pull a shirt on over my head. "So Kenji's gone then, huh? I can't believe he'd just leave like that."

"Why would Kenji be gone?" James asks. "I thought you said you didn't even know if he w—"

"But I thought *you* said—"

We stop. Stare at each other.

James is the first to speak. "I said *Warner* is gone. Everyone is saying he escaped last night."

Just the sound of his name and I'm already pissed off. "Stay here," I say, pointing at James and grabbing my boots.

"But—"

"Don't move until I get back!" I shout before bolting out the door.

That bastard. I can't believe this.

I'm pounding on Castle's door when Ian spots me on his way down the hall.

"He's not in there," Ian says, still walking.

I catch his arm. "Is it true? Did Warner really get out?"

Ian sighs. Shoves his hands into his pockets. Finally, he nods.

I want to put my fist through the wall.

"I gotta go suit up," Ian says, breaking away. "And you should, too. We're heading out after breakfast."

"Are you serious?" I say. "We're still heading out to fight—even with all this shit going on?"

"Of course we are," Ian snaps at me. "You know we can't wait any longer. The supreme isn't going to reschedule his plans to launch an attack on the civilians. It's too late to back out now."

"But what about Warner?" I demand. "We're not going to try and find him?"

"Maybe." Ian shrugs. "See if you can find him on the battlefield."

"Jesus." I'm so filled with rage I can hardly see straight. "I could kill Castle for letting this happen—for being so goddamn soft with him—"

"Rein it in, man." Ian cuts me off. "We've got other problems. And hey"—he grabs my shoulder, looks me in the eye—"you're not the only one who's pissed at Castle. But now's not the time."

I shake him off, shoot him a dark look, and charge back down the hall.

James has all sorts of questions when I get back, but I'm still so angry I'm not ready to deal with him. It doesn't seem to matter; James is stubborn as hell. I'm strapping on holsters and locking my weapons into place and he won't back down.

"But then what did he say?" James is asking. "After you said we should find Warner?"

I adjust my pants, tighten the laces on my boots.

James taps my arm. "Adam." He taps my arm again. "Did he know where Castle was?" Another tap. "Did he say what time you guys had to leave today?" More tapping. "Adam when are y—"

I pick him up and he squeaks; I place him in a far corner of the room.

"Addie—"

I throw a blanket over his head.

James shouts and struggles with the blanket until he manages to pull it off and throw it down. He's red in the face and his fists are clenched and he's finally mad.

I start laughing. I can't help it.

James is so frustrated he has to spit the words out when he speaks. "Kenji said that I have as much right to know what's happening down here as everyone else. Kenji never gets mad when I ask questions. He never ignores me. He's never mean to me, and you're being m-mean to me, and I don't like it when you l-laugh at me—"

James's voice breaks, and it's only then that I look up. I notice the tears streaked across his cheeks.

"Hey," I say, meeting him across the room. "Hey, hey."

I grip his shoulders, drop to one knee. "What's going on? Why the tears? What happened?"

"You're leaving." James hiccups.

"Aw, c'mon," I sigh. "You knew I was leaving, remember? Remember when we talked about this?"

"You're going to die." Another hiccup.

I raise an eyebrow at him. "I didn't know you could tell the future."

"Addie—"

"*Hey—*"

"I don't call you Addie in front of anyone else!" James says, protesting before I have a chance to. "I don't know why it makes you so mad. You said you loved it when Mom called you Addie. Why can't I?"

I sigh again as I get to my feet, mussing his hair on my way up. James makes a strangled sound and jerks away. "What's the problem?" I ask. I pull up my pants leg to attach a semiautomatic to the holster underneath. "I've been a soldier for a long time now. You've always known the risks. What's different all of a sudden?"

James is quiet long enough for me to notice. I look up.

"I want to come with you," he says, wiping his nose with a shaky hand. "I want to fight, too."

My body goes rigid. "We're not having that conversation again."

"But Kenji said—"

"I don't give a rat's ass what Kenji said! You are a ten-year-old *child*," I say. "You are not fighting in any war. Not

118

walking onto any battlefield. Do you understand me?"

James stares at me.

"I said, *Do you understand me?*" I walk right up to him, grab his arms.

James flinches a little. "Yes," he whispers.

"Yes, *what*?"

"Yes, sir," he says, staring at the ground now.

I'm breathing so hard my chest is heaving. "Never again," I say quietly now. "We are never having this conversation. Not ever again."

"Okay, Addie."

I swallow hard.

"I'm sorry, Addie."

"Get your shoes on." I stare at the wall. "It's time for breakfast."

TWO

"Hi."

Juliette is standing next to my table, staring at me like she might be nervous. Like we've never done this before.

"Hey," I say.

Just seeing her face still makes my chest ache, but the truth is, I have no idea what's going on between us anymore. I promised her I would find a way through this—and I've been training like hell, I really have—but after last night, I'm not gonna lie: I'm a little freaked out. Touching her is more serious than I ever thought it was.

She could've killed Kenji. I'm still not sure she hasn't.

But even after all this, I still want a future with her. I want to know that one day we'll be able to settle somewhere safe and be together in peace. I'm not ready to give up on that dream yet. I'm not ready to give up on us.

I nod at an empty seat. "You want to sit down?"

She does.

We sit in silence a little while, her poking at her food, me at mine. We usually eat the same thing every morning: a spoonful of rice, a bowl of vegetable broth, a chunk of rock-hard bread, and, on good days, a little cup of pudding. It's not amazing, but it gets the job done, and we're usually grateful for it. But today neither one of us seems to have an appetite.

Or a voice.

I sigh and look away. I don't know why it's so hard to talk to her this morning—maybe it's the lack of Kenji—but things feel different between us lately. I want to be with her so badly, but being with her has never felt more danger-ous than it does now. Every day we feel further apart. And sometimes I think the harder I try to hold on, the more she tries to break away.

I wish James would hurry up and grab his breakfast. Having him here might make this easier. I sit up and look around the room, only to spot him talking with a group of his friends. I try to wave him over, but he's laughing at something and doesn't even notice me. The kid is kind of amazing. He's such a social guy—and so popular around here—that sometimes I wonder where he got it from. In many ways he's the exact opposite of me. He likes to let a lot of people in; I like to keep most people out.

Juliette's the only real exception to that rule.

I look back at her and notice the red rims around her eyes as they dart across the dining hall. She looks both wide awake and crazy tired and she can't seem to sit still; her foot is tapping fast under the table and her hands are trembling a little.

"Hey are you okay?" I ask.

"Yes, absolutely," she says too quickly. But she's shaking her head.

"Did you, um, get enough sleep last night?"

"Yes," she says, repeating the word a few times. She does that occasionally—repeats the same word over and over again. I'm not sure she's even aware of it.

"Did you sleep well?" she asks. Her fingers drum against the table, then against her arms. She keeps glancing around the room. She doesn't even wait for me to respond before she says, "Have you heard anything about Kenji yet?"

That's when I understand.

Of course she's not okay. Of course she didn't get any sleep last night. Last night she almost killed one of her closest friends. She'd just started trusting herself and not being afraid of herself; now she's back to where she started. Shit. I'm already sorry I even brought it up.

"No, not yet." I cringe. "But," I say, hoping to change the subject, "I have heard that people are pretty pissed at Castle about what happened with Warner." I clear my throat. "Did you hear about him breaking out of here?"

Juliette drops her spoon.

It clatters to the floor and she doesn't seem to notice. "Yes," she says quietly. She's blinking at her water cup, holding her napkin in her hands, folding and refolding it. "People were talking about it in the halls. Do they know how he escaped?"

"I don't think so." I frown at her.

"Oh." She says that a few times, too.

She sounds strange. Scared, even. Juliette has always been a little different from everyone else—she was like a

crazed, skittish kitten when I first saw her in that cell—
but she'd been getting a lot better over the last few months.
Once she finally started trusting me, things changed. She
evolved. She started talking (and eating) more and even got
a little cocky. I loved seeing her come back to life. I loved
being with her, watching her find herself.

I think this experience with Kenji really set her back.

I can tell she's only halfway here, because her eyes are
unfocused and her hands are moving mechanically. She does
this a lot. It's like sometimes she just disappears, retreats
into a corner of her brain and stays there awhile, thinking
about something she'll never talk about. She's acting a lot
like her old self right now, and right now she's eating the
cold rice on her plate one grain at a time, counting each bite
under her breath.

I'm about to try speaking to her again when James finally
comes back to the table. I stand up immediately, grateful for
the opportunity to shake off the awkward. "Hey buddy—
why don't we go have a proper good-bye?"

"Oh," James says, sliding his tray onto the table. "Okay,
sure." He glances at me before glancing at Juliette, who's
now chewing a grain of rice very carefully.

"Hi," he says to her.

Juliette blinks a few times, her face breaking into a wide
smile the moment she notices him. It changes her, those
smiles. And those are the moments that kill me a little.

"Hi," she says, so happy so suddenly you'd think James
had hung the moon for her. "How are you? Did you sleep

well? Would you like to sit down? I was just having some rice; would you like some rice?"

James is already blushing. He'd probably eat his own hair if she asked him to. I roll my eyes and drag him away, telling Juliette we'll be right back.

She nods. I look over my shoulder as we walk away and notice that she doesn't seem to mind sitting alone for a little while. She stabs at something on her plate and misses, and that's the last I see of her before we turn the corner.

THREE

"What's going on? Why do we need to talk?" More questions from James. He's a freaking question machine. "Is everything okay? Can you tell Juliette not to eat my breakfast?" He cranes his neck to catch a glimpse of her, still sitting at the table. "Sometimes she eats my pudding."

"Hey," I say, grabbing hold of his shoulders. "Look at me."

James turns to face me. "What's wrong, Addie?" He searches my eyes. "You're not really going to die, are you?"

"I don't know," I tell him. "Maybe, maybe not."

"Don't say that," he says quietly, dropping his gaze. "Don't say that. It's not nice to talk like that."

"James."

He looks up again, slowly this time.

I drop to my knees and pull him close, resting my forehead against his. I'm staring at the floor, and I know he is, too. I can hear our hearts racing in the silence.

"I love you," I finally say to him. "You know that, right? You always come first. Everything I do is to take care of you. To protect you. To provide for you."

James nods.

"It's you first," I say to him. "It's always you first and

everyone else second. And that's never going to change. Okay?"

James nods again. A tear falls on the floor between us. "Okay, Addie."

"Come here," I whisper, tugging him into my arms. "We're going to be okay."

James clings to me, acting more like a child than he has in a long time, and I'm happy to see it. Sometimes I worry he's growing up way too fast in this shitty world, and though I know I can't protect him from everything, I still try. He's been the only constant in my life for as long as I can remember; I think it'd rip me apart if anything happened to him.

I'll never love anyone the way I love this kid.

FOUR

After breakfast, the dining hall is practically empty. James had to report to the Safe Room with the other kids—and the elderly—staying behind, and everyone else is getting ready to head out. Some families are still saying final good-byes. Juliette and I have been avoiding eye contact for a few minutes now. She's staring at her hands, studying her fingers like she's checking to make sure they're still there.

"Well damn. Who died?"

Holy hell. That voice. That face.

Impossible.

"Holy crap. Holy *shit*." I'm on my feet.

"Good to see you too, Kent." Kenji smiles wide and nods at me. He looks like hell. Tired eyes, pale face, hands shaking just a little as he holds on to the table. And what's worse is that he's already suited up—like he actually thinks he's heading out onto the battlefield. "You ready to kick some ass today?"

I'm still staring at him in amazement, trying to find a way to respond, when Juliette jumps up and practically tackles him. Just a hug, really, but yikes.

A little too soon for that, I think.

"*Whoa*—hey—thank you, yeah—that's—uh—" Kenji

clears his throat. He tries to be nice about it, but it's clear he's trying to back away from Juliette, and yeah, she notices. Her face falls and she goes pale, her eyes wide. She hides her hands behind her back, even though she's wearing her gloves. There's really no obvious threat to Kenji right now, but I understand his hesitation.

The dude almost died. He tried to break up a fight at the same time Juliette did, and *bam*, he went down in an instant. It was scary as hell—and even though I know Juliette didn't *mean* to do it, there's really no other explanation. It had to have been her.

"Yeah, um, maybe you should hold off on touching me for a little while, yeah?" Kenji is smiling—again, nice guy—but no one's buying it. "I'm not too steady on my feet just yet."

Juliette looks so mortified it breaks my heart. She's trying so hard to be okay—to make all this shit be okay—but sometimes it's like the world just won't let her. The hits keep coming, and she keeps hurting. I hate it.

I have to say something.

"It wasn't her," I say to Kenji. I shoot him a sharp look. *Leave her alone*, I mouth. "You know she didn't even touch you."

"I *don't* know that, actually," Kenji says, ignoring my more subtle hints to change the subject. "And it's not like I'm blaming her—I'm just saying maybe she's projecting and doesn't know it, okay? Because last I checked, I don't think we have any other explanations for what happened last night. It sure as hell wasn't you," he says to me, "and shit, for all we know, Warner being able to touch Juliette could just be a fluke. We don't know anything about him yet." A pause. "Right? Unless Warner pulled some kind of magical rabbit out of his ass while I was busy being dead last night?"

I frown. Look away.

"Right," Kenji says. "That's what I thought. So. I think it's best if, unless absolutely necessary, I stay away." He turns to Juliette. "Right? No offense, right? I mean I did nearly just die. I think you could cut me some slack."

"Yeah, of course," Juliette says quietly. She tries to laugh but it comes out all wrong. I wish I could reach for her; I wish I could wrap her up in my arms. I want to protect her—I want to be able to take care of her, but that seems impossible now.

"So *anyway*," Kenji says. "When are we leaving?"

That gets my attention.

"You're insane," I say to him. "You're not going any-where."

"Bullshit I'm not."

"You can barely stand up on your own!"

"I'd rather die out there than sit in here like some kind of idiot."

"Kenji—," Juliette tries to say.

"Heeeeey, so I heard through the very loud grapevine that Warner got his ass the hell out of here last night." Kenji looks at us. "What's that about?"

"Yeah," I say, my mood darkening. "Who even knows. I

never thought it was a good idea to keep him hostage here. It was an even stupider idea to trust him."

Kenji raises an eyebrow. "So first you insult my idea, and then you insult Castle's, huh?"

"They were bad calls," I say to him, refusing to back down. "Bad ideas. Now we have to pay for it." It was Kenji's idea to take Warner hostage, and Castle's idea to let him out of his room. And now we're all suffering. Sometimes I think this whole movement is led by a bunch of idiots.

"Well how was I supposed to know Anderson would be so willing to let his own son rot in hell?"

I wince involuntarily.

The reminder of my father and what he'd be willing to do to his own son is too much for me this morning. I swallow back the bile inching up my throat.

Kenji notices. "Oh, hey—I'm sorry man—I didn't mean to say it like that—"

"Forget it," I say to him. I'm glad Kenji's not dead, but sometimes all I really want to do is kick his ass. "Maybe you should get back to the medical wing. We're leaving soon."

"I'm not going anywhere but *out of here*."

"Kenji please—" Juliette again.

"Nope."

"You're being unreasonable. This isn't a joke," she says to him. "People are going to die today."

Kenji laughs at her. "I'm sorry, are you trying to teach *me* about the realities of war?" He shakes his head. "Are you forgetting that I was a soldier in Warner's army? Do you have any idea how much crazy shit we've seen?" He gestures to me. "I know exactly what to expect today. Warner was *insane*. If Anderson is even twice as bad as his son, then we are diving right into a bloodbath. I can't leave you guys hanging like that."

Juliette is frozen, her lips just parted, her eyes wide and horrified. Her reaction feels a little exaggerated.

There's definitely something wrong with her today.

I know part of what she's feeling has to do with Kenji, but suddenly I'm not sure if there isn't something else. Something she's not telling me.

I can't read her clearly.

Then again, I feel like I haven't been able to read her clearly for a while now.

"Was he really that bad . . . ?" Juliette asks.

"Who?" Kenji and I ask at the same time.

"Warner," she says. "Was he really that ruthless?"

God, she's so obsessed with him. She has some weird fascination with his twisted life that I don't understand, and it makes me crazy. I can already feel myself getting angry, annoyed—*jealous*, even—which is ridiculous. Warner isn't even human; I shouldn't be comparing myself to him. Besides, she's not his type at all. He'd probably eat her alive.

Kenji, however, doesn't seem to have my problem. He's laughing so hard he's practically wheezing. "Ruthless? Juliette, the guy is sick. He's an animal. I don't think he even knows what it means to be human. If there's a hell out there, I'm guessing it was designed especially for him."

I catch a glimpse of Juliette's face just before I hear a rush of footsteps charging down the hall. We all glance at one another, but I look at Juliette for a second longer, wishing I could read her mind. I have no idea what she's thinking or why she still looks so horrified. I want to talk to her in private—find out what's going on—but then Kenji nods at me, and I know I have to clear my head.

It's time to go.

We all get to our feet.

"Hey—so, does Castle know what you're doing?" I ask Kenji. "I don't think he'd be okay with you going out there today."

"Castle wants me to be happy," Kenji says. "And I won't be happy if I stay here. I've got work to do. People to save. Ladies to impress. He'd respect that."

"What about everyone else?" Juliette asks him. "Everyone was so worried about you—have you even seen them yet? To at least tell them you're okay?"

"Nah," Kenji says. "They'd probably shit a brick if they knew I was going up. I thought it'd be safer to keep it quiet. I don't want to freak anyone out. And Sonya and Sara—poor kids—they're passed the hell out. It's my fault they're so exhausted, and they're still talking about heading out today. They want to fight even though they're going to have a lot of work to do once we're done with Anderson's army. I've been trying to convince them to stay here, but they can be so damn stubborn. They need to save their strength," he says, "and they've already wasted too much of it on me."

"It's not a *waste*—," she says.

"Anywaaay," Kenji says. "Can we please get going? I know you're all about hunting down Anderson," he says to me, "but personally? I would love to catch Warner. Put a bullet through that worthless piece of crap and be done with it."

I'm about to laugh—finally, someone who agrees with me—when I see Juliette double over. She steadies herself quickly enough, but she's blinking fast and breathing hard, eyes up at the ceiling.

"Hey—you okay?" I pull her to the side and study her face. She scares the shit out of me sometimes. I worry about her almost as much as I do about James.

"I'm okay," she says too many times. Nodding and shaking her head over and over again. "I just didn't get enough sleep last night, but I'll be fine."

I hesitate. "Are you sure?"

"I'm positive," she says. And then she grabs my shirt, eyes wild. "Hey—just be careful out there, okay?"

I nod, more confused by the second. "Yeah. You too."

"Let's go let's go let's go!" Kenji interrupts us. "Today is our day to die, ladies."

I relax and shove him a little. It's nice to have him around to break up the monotony in this place.

Kenji punches me in the arm. "So now you're abusing the crippled kid, huh?"

I laugh, flip him off.

"Save your angst for the battlefield, bro." He grins. "You're going to need it."

FIVE

It's raining like hell.

It's cold and wet and muddy and shitty and I hate this. I scowl at Kenji and Juliette, jealous of their fancy suits. Those things are built to give them protection from this crazy winter weather. I should've asked for one.

I'm already freezing my ass off.

We're at the clearing, the barren stretch at the entrance of Omega Point, and most everyone else has scattered. Our only defense is guerrilla warfare, so we've been divided into groups. Me; an ill, barely-able-to-walk-straight Kenji; and Juliette (who's officially locked herself in her own head today)—*this* is our team.

Yeah, I'm definitely worried.

Anyway, at least Kenji is doing his thing: we're already invisible. But now it's time to find the action and join in. The sound of gunshots rings out loud and clear, so we've already got a direction to move in. No one speaks, but we already know the rules: we fight to protect the innocent, and we fight to survive. That's it.

The rain is really messing things up, though. It's falling harder and faster now, pelting me in the face and blurring my vision. I can hardly see straight. I try to wipe the water from my eyes but it's no use. There's too much.

I do know we're getting closer to the compounds, so at least there's that. The outline of the buildings comes into focus and I feel myself getting excited. I'm armed to the teeth and ready to fight—ready to do whatever is necessary to take down The Reestablishment—but I'm not gonna lie: I'm still a little worried we've got a handicap.

Juliette has never done this before.

If it were up to me, she'd be back on base with James where I know she'd be safe, but she wouldn't listen to me even if I asked her to. Kenji and Castle are always blowing smoke up her ass when they shouldn't, and honestly? It's dangerous. It's not good to make her think she can do this kind of thing when really, it'll probably get her killed. She's not a soldier; she doesn't know how to fight; and she has no idea how to use her powers, not really, which makes things even worse. It's basically like giving a toddler a stick of dynamite and telling him to walk into a fire.

So yeah, I'm worried. I'm really worried something is going to happen to her. And maybe to us, by extension.

But no one ever listens to me, so here we are.

I sigh and forge ahead, irritated, until I hear a piercing scream in the distance. High alert. Kenji squeezes my hand and I squeeze back to let him know I understand.

The compounds are straight ahead, and Kenji pulls us forward until we're standing flush against the back wall of a unit. There's just enough overhang from the roof to keep the rain off. It's just my shitty luck that we're doing this on a rainy day. My clothes are so wet I feel like I've pissed my pants.

Kenji elbows me, just a little, and I'm paying attention again. I hear the sound of a door slam open and I go rigid; I reach for my gun automatically. It feels like I've been through this a million times before, but it's never something I get used to.

"This is the last of them," a voice shouts. "She was hiding out over here."

A soldier is dragging a woman out of her home and she won't stop screaming. My heart speeds up, and I grip my gun more tightly. It's sick, the way some of the soldiers treat the civilians. I get that he's under orders—I really do—but the poor woman is begging for mercy and he's dragging her by the hair and shouting at her to shut up.

Kenji is barely breathing next to me. I glance Juliette's way before I realize we're still invisible, and as I turn my head, I catch a glimpse of another soldier. He jogs over from across the field and shoots the first guy a signal. Not the kind of signal I was hoping for.

Shit.

"Toss her in with everyone else," the other soldier is saying now. "And then we'll call this area clear." Suddenly he's gone, around the corner, and no one's left but us, one soldier, and the lady he's holding hostage. Other soldiers must've rounded up the remaining civilians before we got here.

Then the woman loses it. She's completely hysterical and

doesn't seem to be in control of her body anymore. She's gone totally animal, screeching and clawing and flailing, tripping over her own feet. She's asking after her husband and her daughter and I almost have to close my eyes. It's hard to watch this stuff when I already know what's going to happen. War never gets easier when you don't agree with what's going on. Sometimes I let myself get excited about going to battle—I have to convince myself I'm doing something worthwhile—but fighting another soldier is way easier than dealing with some lady who's about to watch her daughter get shot in the head.

Juliette will probably puke.

The action is so close to us now that I instinctively press my back into the wall, forgetting again that we're invisible. The soldier grabs the lady and slams her body against the outside of the unit, and I feel the three of us collectively freak out for a second, calming down just in time to watch the soldier press the barrel of his gun to the lady's neck and say, "If you don't shut up I'll shoot you right now." What an asshole.

The lady faints.

The soldier doesn't seem to care. He pulls her out of sight—in the same direction his comrade went—and that's our cue to follow. I can hear Kenji cursing under his breath. He's got a soft stomach, that guy. He was always soft when it came to this stuff. I met him for the first time on one of our rounds; when we came back, Kenji lost his shit. Just completely lost it. They put him in solitary confinement for a little while, and after that he kept his emotional breakdowns to a minimum. Most soldiers know better than to complain out loud. I should've known then that Kenji wasn't really one of us.

I shudder against the cold.

We're still following the soldier, but it's hard to stay too close to him in this weather. Visibility is shot, and the wind is blowing the rain around so hard it's almost like we're trapped in a hurricane. This is going to get ugly really quickly.

Then, a small voice: "What do you think is going on?"

Juliette.

Of course she has no idea what's happening—why would she?

The smart thing to do would be to hide her somewhere. Keep her safe. Out of danger. A weak link can bring everything down with it, and I don't think this is the time to be taking chances. But Kenji, as usual, doesn't seem to agree. Apparently he doesn't mind making time to give Juliette a tutorial on being at war in Sector 45.

"They're herding them up," Kenji explains. "They're creating groups of people to kill all at once."

"The woman—," Juliette says.

"Yeah." Kenji cuts her off. "Yeah," Kenji says again. "She and whoever else they think might be connected to the protests," he says. "They don't just kill the inciters. They kill the friends and the family members, too. It's the best way to keep people in line. It never fails to scare the shit out of the few left alive."

I have to jump in before Juliette asks any more questions. Those soldiers aren't going to wait patiently for us to get there—we have to make a move now, and we need a plan. "There has to be a way to get them out of there," I say. "Maybe we can take out the soldiers in charge—"

"Yeah but listen, you guys know I'm going to have to let go of you, right?" Kenji asks. "I'm already kind of losing strength; my energy is fading faster than normal. So you'll be visible. You'll be a clearer target."

"But what other choice do we have?" Juliette asks.

She's like the second coming of James. I feel for my gun, flexing and unflexing my fingers around it. We need to get going.

We need to move *now*.

"We could try to take them out sniper-style," Kenji says. "We don't have to engage in direct combat. We have that option." He pauses. "Juliette, you've never been in this kind of situation before. I want you to know I'd respect your decision to stay out of the direct line of fire. Not everyone can stomach what we might see if we follow those soldiers. There's no shame or blame in that."

Yes. Good. Let her stay behind where she won't get hurt.

"I'll be okay," she says.

I swear under my breath.

"Just—all right—but don't be afraid to use your abilities

140

to defend yourself," Kenji says. He seems a little nervous about her, too. "I know you're all weird about not wanting to hurt people or whatever, but these guys aren't messing around. They *will* try to kill you."

"Right," Juliette says. "Yeah. Let's go."

SIX

Juliette shouldn't have to see this.

Six soldiers have rounded up almost thirty civilians—a mix of men, women, and children—and they're going to kill them. It's basically a firing squad. They'll just go down the row, *pop pop pop*, and then drag the dead bodies away. Put them into an incinerator. Clean it up, nice and simple.

It's disgusting.

I'm not sure what the soldiers are waiting for, though. Maybe they need final approval from somewhere, but there's a slight delay as they talk amongst themselves. It's raining really freaking hard, so that might have something to do with it. Honestly, they might not even be able to see where they're shooting. We should be taking advantage of this opportunity. This weather might end up helping us out in the end.

I squint against the rain and take a closer look at the people, trying hard not to lose my head. They're not doing too well, and I'm not either, to be honest. Some are pretty hysterical, and it makes me wonder how I would do in a situation like that. Maybe I'd be like that guy in the middle, standing there with absolutely no expression on his face. He looks almost like he's accepted what's going to happen, and somehow, his certainty hits me even harder than the tears.

A shot rings out.

Dammit.

A guy on the far left falls to the ground and I'm shaking with anger. These people need our help. We can't just hang back and watch thirty unarmed, innocent people get killed when we could find a way to save them. We're supposed to be *doing something*, but we're standing here for some bullshit reason I can't understand because Juliette is scared or Kenji is sick and I guess the truth is we're just a bunch of crappy teenagers, two of whom can barely stand up straight or fire a weapon, and it's unacceptable. I'm just about to say something—I'm about to yell something, actually—when Kenji lets go of my hand.

About goddamn time.

We charge straight ahead and my gun is already up and aimed. I spot the soldier who fired the first shot and I know I need to fire; there's no room for hesitation. I get lucky: he goes down instantly. Five more soldiers to take out—soldiers I'm hoping I won't recognize—and I'm doing my best, but it's not easy. It was pure luck that got me that first target; it's almost impossible to shoot well in this weather. I can barely see where I'm going, much less where I'm shooting, but I drop to the ground just in time to avoid a stray bullet. At least the rain is making it hard for them to take us out, too.

Kenji is making miracles happen today.

He's invisible now, and working fast. He's staying sharp despite being injured, and he's just a part of the wind, taking out three soldiers in one go. Two soldiers are left and they're distracted by Kenji's dance just long enough for me to take one down. One more left and I'm about to take him out, too, when I see Juliette shoot him from behind.

Not bad.

Kenji reappears just then and he starts bellowing for the civilians to follow us back to shelter, and Juliette and I join in, doing what we can to get them to safety as quickly as possible. There are a few compounds still standing, and they should be enough. The civilians can get inside and away from the battle—as well as the storm brewing in the sky. And even though their gratitude is touching, we can't stop long enough to talk to them. We have to settle them back into their homes, and then keep moving.

It's what I've always done.

Always keep moving.

I glance at Juliette as we run, wondering how she's holding up, and for a second I'm confused; I can't tell if she's crying or if it's just the rain streaking down her cheeks. I'm hoping she'll be okay, though. It kills me to see her deal with this. I wish she didn't have to.

We're running again, charging through the compounds now that we've gotten the civilians back into their homes. This was just a stop on the way to our final destination; we haven't even reached the battlefield yet, where Point men and women are already trying to keep Reestablishment soldiers from slaughtering innocent civilians. Things are about to get much, much worse.

Kenji is pulling us through the half-demolished land-scape. I know we're getting closer to the action now because there's so much more devastation here: units falling apart and half on fire, their contents strewn everywhere. Ripped couches and broken lamps, clothes and shoes and fallen bodies to step over. The compounds feel like they could stretch on forever, and the farther we go, the uglier it gets.

"We're close!" I shout to Kenji.

He nods, and I'm surprised he even heard me.

I hear a familiar sound. "Tanks!" I call out to him. "You hear that?"

Kenji shoots me a bleak look and nods. "Let's move!" he says, making a motion with his hand. "We're not far now!"

It's a fight to get to the fight, the wind whistling hard in our ears and slapping sharply against our faces, angry raindrops pelting our skin, soaking our hair. I'm frozen to the bone but there's no time to be bothered by it. I've got adrenaline, and that'll have to be enough for now.

The earth shakes under our feet as a harsh, booming sound explodes in the sky. In an instant the horizon is lit on fire, flames roaring in the distance. Someone is dropping bombs, and that means we're already screwed. My heart is beating fast and hard, and I'd never admit it out loud, but I'm starting to get nervous.

I glance at Juliette again. I know she's probably scared, and I want to reassure her—to tell her everything is going to be okay—but she doesn't look my way. She's in another world, her eyes cold and sharp, focused on the fire in the distance. She looks different—a little scary, even. Somehow, that worries me even more.

I'm paying such close attention to her that I almost trip; the ground is slick underfoot and I'm up to my ankles in mud. I pull my legs free as we forge ahead, gun steady in my hands, and focus. This is it. This is where it's all about to get very serious, and I know enough about war to be honest with myself: I might walk onto that battlefield with a beating heart and be dragged off with a dead one.

I take a deep breath as we approach, three invisible kids walking through the compounds. We make our way over fallen units, broken glass from shattered windows; we side-step the garbage strewn about and try not to hear the sound of people screaming. And I don't know about the rest of us, but I'm doing my best to fight the urge to turn around and run back to where we started.

Suddenly James is the only person on my mind.

SEVEN

Shit.

This is even worse than I was expecting. There are fallen bodies everywhere, collapsed and piled together and bleeding into one another. It's almost impossible to distinguish arms from legs, enemies from allies. Blood and rain are mixing together and flooding the ground, and suddenly my boots are slick with mud and the blood of someone else— dead or alive, I don't know.

It takes just a split second for enemy combatants to realize we're new to the battlefield; when they do, they don't hesitate. We're already under siege, and I glance back just in time to catch a glimpse of Juliette and Kenji still making their way forward before I feel something sharp slam into my back. I spin around, and one sharp crack later my soldier's got a broken jaw. He doubles over and reaches for his gun and I beat him to it. Now he's down and out, and I'm already moving on to the next one.

We're all so jam-packed together that hand-to-hand combat seems unavoidable; I duck to avoid a right hook and punch the opposing soldier in the gut on my way up, grabbing a knife from my belt to follow through. In, up, twist, and he's done. I yank my knife out of his chest as he falls.

Someone charges at me from behind and I turn to meet him when suddenly he's coughing up blood and falling to his knees.

Kenji saved my ass.

He's on the move and moving well, still not letting his injury cripple him. We're fighting together, he and I, and I can feel his movements beside me. We shout warnings to each other, helping each other when we can, and we're actually doing okay, making our way through the madness, when I hear Kenji shouting my name, his voice scared and urgent.

Suddenly I'm invisible and Kenji is screaming at me about Juliette and I don't know what's happening but I'm freaking out and I know now's not the time to ask questions. We fight our way back to the front and jet toward the road, Kenji's panicked voice telling me he saw Juliette go down and get dragged away, and that's all I need to hear. I'm one part furious and one part terrified, and the two are having a battle of their own in my mind.

I knew this would happen.

I knew she never should've come with us. I knew she should've stayed behind. She's not built for this—she's not strong enough to be on the battlefield. She would've been so much safer if she'd stayed behind. *Why does no one ever listen to me?*

Dammit.

I want to scream.

When we reach the road, Kenji pulls me back, and

though we're out of breath and barely able to speak, we catch a glimpse of Juliette as she's loaded into the back of a tank, her body limp and heavy as they drag her inside.

It's over in a matter of seconds. They're already driving away.

Juliette is gone.

My chest cracks open.

Kenji has a firm hand on my shoulder and I realize I'm saying "Oh God, oh God" over and over again when Kenji has the decency to shake some sense into me.

"Get your shit together," he says. "We need to go after her!"

My legs are unsteady, but I know he's right. "Where do you think they went?"

"They're probably carting her back to base—"

"Dammit. Of course! Warner—"

"Wants her back." Kenji nods. "That was probably his team he sent to collect her." He swears under his breath. "Only good thing about that is we know he doesn't want her dead."

I grit my teeth to keep from losing my mind. "All right then; let's go."

God, I can't wait to get my hands on that psychopath. I'm going to enjoy killing him. Slowly. Carefully. Cutting him to pieces one finger at a time.

But Kenji hesitates, and I stare at him.

"What?" I ask.

"I can't project, bro. My energy is shot." He sighs. "I'm

sorry. My body is seriously jacked up right now."

Shit. "Contingency plan?"

"We can avoid the main roads," he says. "Take the back route and head to base on our own. It'd be easier to track the tank, but if we do, you'll be in plain sight. It's your call."

I frown. "Yeah, I vote for the plan that doesn't get me killed instantly."

Kenji grins. "Okay then. Let's go get our girl back."

"*My* girl," I correct him. "She's my girl."

Kenji snorts as we head in the direction of the compounds. "Right. Minus the part where she's not actually your girl. Not anymore."

"Shut up."

"Uh-huh."

"Whatever."

EIGHT

It takes us a while to get back to base, because we have to be hyperaware of my visibility. We're slower, more cautious, and careful to take our time hiding inside and around abandoned units every hundred yards or so, just to make sure the coast is clear around every corner. But when we're finally approaching base, shit kicks into high gear.

We weren't the only ones taking the back route.

Castle, Ian, Alia, and Lily flipped out when they saw us; they were hiding inside a unit we thought for sure was empty. They jumped out at us from behind a bed, which made me nearly piss my pants. We only had a moment to explain what had happened before Castle was sharing his own story.

They got Brendan and Winston back—broke them out of Sector 45 just as they'd originally planned—but the two of them were in bad shape when Castle found them.

"We think they'll be okay," Castle is saying, "but we have to get them to the girls as soon as possible. I'm hoping they'll be able to help."

"The girls are on the battlefield," Kenji says, eyes wide. "I have no idea where. They insisted on fighting today."

Castle's face falls, and though he doesn't say it out loud,

it's clear he's suddenly very worried.

"Where are they now?" I ask. "Brendan and Winston?"

"Hiding," Castle says.

"What?" Kenji looks around. "Why? Why aren't you taking them back to Point?"

Castle goes pale.

It's Lily who speaks. "We heard whispers while we were on base breaking them out," she says. "Whispers of what the soldiers are going to do next."

"They're mobilizing for an air assault," Ian cuts in. "We just heard they're going to bomb Omega Point. We were still trying to figure out what we should do when we heard someone coming, and jumped in here"—he nods around the unit—"to hide."

"What?" Kenji panics. "But—how do you—"

"It's definite," Castle says. His eyes are deep and tortured. Terrified. "I heard the orders myself. They're hoping that if they hit it with enough firepower, everything underground will just collapse in on itself."

"But sir, no one knows the exact location of Omega Point, it's not possible—"

"It is," Alia says. I've never heard her speak before, and I'm surprised by the softness of her voice. "They tortured the information out of some of our own."

"On the battlefield," Ian says. "Just before killing them."

Kenji looks like he might throw up. "We have to go right now," he says, his voice high and sharp. "We have to get everyone out of there—all the ones we left behind—"

Only then does it hit me.

"*James.*"

I don't recognize my own voice. The horror, the panic, the dread that floods my body is something I've never felt— never known before. Not like this. "We have to get James!" I'm shouting, and Kenji is trying to calm me down, but this time I can't listen. I don't care if I have to go alone; I'm getting my brother out of there. "Let's go!" I bark at Kenji. "We have to get a tank and get back to base as soon as possible—"

"But what about Juliette?" Kenji asks. "Maybe we can split up—I can head back to Point with Castle and Alia; you can stay here with Ian and Lily—"

"No. I have to get James. I have to be there. I have to be the one to get him—"

"But Juliette—"

"You said yourself that Warner isn't going to kill her— she'll be okay there for a little while. But right now they're going to blow up Omega Point, and James—and everyone else—is going to die. We have to go *now*—"

"Maybe I can stay here and look for Juliette, and you guys can go—"

"Juliette will be fine. She's not in any immediate danger here—Warner isn't going to hurt her—"

"But—"

"Kenji, *please!*" I'm desperate now and I don't care. "We need as many people at Omega Point as possible. There are tons of people left behind, and they don't stand a chance if we don't get to them now."

Kenji stares at me for just a moment longer before he nods. "You guys go grab Brendan and Winston," he says to Castle and the three others. "Kent and I will commandeer a tank and meet you back here. We'll do everything we can to get back to Point as soon as possible."

The second everyone is gone, I grab Kenji by the arm. "If anything happens to James—"

"We're going to do everything we can, I promise—"

"That's not good enough for me—I need to go get him—I need to go right now—"

"You *can't* go right now," Kenji snaps. "Save your stupid for later, Kent. Now, more than ever, you need to stay in control. If you go crazy and head back to Point on foot with no regard for your own safety, you'll be dead before you even get there, and any chance of saving James will be lost. You want to keep your little brother alive? Make sure you don't kill yourself while you're trying to save him."

I feel like my throat is closing up. "He can't die," I say, my voice breaking. "I can't be the reason he dies, Kenji—I can't. . . ."

Kenji blinks fast, forcing back his own emotion. "I know, man. But I can't think like that right now. We have to keep moving. . . ."

Kenji is still talking, but I can hardly hear him.

James.

Oh God.

What have I done.

NINE

I have no idea how we all fit inside this tank. We're eight people jammed into cramped quarters, sitting on laps, and no one even cares. The tension is so thick it's practically its own person, taking up a seat we don't have to spare. I can barely think straight.

I'm trying to breathe, trying to stay calm, and I can't.

The planes are already overhead, and I feel sick in a way I don't know how to explain. It's deeper than my stomach. Bigger than my heart. More overwhelming than just my mind. It's like fear has become me; it wears my body like an old suit.

Fear is all I have left now.

I think we all feel it. Kenji is driving this tank, somehow still able to function in the face of all this, but no one else is moving. Not speaking. Not even breathing too loudly.

I feel so sick.

Oh God, oh God.

Drive faster, I want to say, but then, actually, I don't. I don't know if I want to hurry up or slow down. I don't know what will hurt more. I watched my own mother die, and, somehow, it didn't hurt as much as this.

I throw up then.

All over the floor mats.

The dead body of my ten-year-old brother.

I'm dry-heaving, wiping my mouth on my shirt.

Will it hurt when he dies? Will he feel it? Will he be killed instantly, or will he be impaled—injured, somehow—and die slowly? Will he bleed to death all alone? My ten-year-old brother?

I'm holding fast to the dashboard, trying to steady my heart, my breathing. It's impossible. The tears are falling fast now, my shoulders shaking, my body breaking. The planes get louder as they come closer. I can hear it now. We all can.

We're not even there yet.

We hear the bombs explode far off in the distance, and that's when I feel it: the bones inside of me fracture, little earthquakes breaking me apart.

The tank stops.

There's no going forward anymore. There's no one and nothing to get to, and we all know it. The bombs keep falling and I hear the explosions echoing the sounds of my own sobs, loud and gasping in the silence. I have nothing left now.

Nothing left.

Nothing so precious as my own flesh and blood.

I've just dropped my head into my hands when a scream pierces the quiet.

"Kenji! Look!"

It's Alia, shrieking from the backseat as she throws the

door open and jumps out. I follow her with my eyes and only then see what she saw, and it takes just seconds before I'm out the door and bolting past her, falling to my knees in front of the one person I never thought I'd see, not ever again.

TEN

I'm almost too overcome to speak.

James is standing in front of me, sobbing, and I don't know if I'm dreaming.

"James?" I hear Kenji say. I look back to see almost everyone has gotten out of the tank now. "Is that you, buddy?"

"Addie, I'm s-sorry," he hiccups. "I know you s-said—you s-said I wasn't supposed to fight, but I couldn't stay behind and I had to l-leave—"

I pull him into my arms, clutching him tight, hardly able to breathe.

"I wanted to f-fight with you," he stammers. "I didn't w-want to be a baby. I wanted t-to h-help—"

"Shhhh," I say to him. "It's okay, James. It's okay. We're okay. It's going to be okay."

"But Addie," he says, "you don't know what h-happened—I'd only been gone a little while and then I saw the p-planes—"

I shush him again and tell him it's okay. That we know what happened. That he's safe now.

"I'm sorry I couldn't h-help you," he says, pulling back to look me in the eye, his cheeks a splotchy red and streaked with tears. "I know you said I shouldn't, but I really w-wanted to h-help—"

I pick him up, cradling his body in my arms as I carry him back to the tank, and only then realize that the wet stain down the front of his pants isn't from the rain.

James must've been terrified. He must've been scared out of his mind and still, he snuck out of Omega Point because he wanted to help. Because he wanted to fight alongside us.

I could kill him for it.

But damn if he's not one of the bravest people I've ever known.

ELEVEN

Once we're back in the tank, we realize we have no idea what to do.

Nowhere to go.

The depth of what's happened has only begun to hit us. And just because I was able to salvage a bit of good news from the wreckage doesn't mean there isn't a lot left to grieve.

Castle is practically comatose.

Kenji is the only one who's still trying to keep us alive. He's the only one with any sense of self-preservation left, and I think it's *because* of Castle. Because no one is leading us anymore, and someone has to step up.

But even with Kenji doing his best to keep us focused, few of us are responding. The day has come to a close much more quickly than we could've expected, and the sun is setting fast, plunging us all into darkness.

We're tired, we're broken, and we can no longer function.

Sleep, it seems, is the only thing that will come.

TWELVE

James stirs in my arms.

I'm awake in an instant, blinking fast and looking around to find everyone else still asleep. The sun slits open the horizon to let the light out, and the morning is so still, and so quiet, it seems impossible there's ever been anything wrong.

The truth, however, comes back too quickly.

It's bricks on my chest, pressure in my lungs, aches in my joints, and metal in my mouth—reminders of the long day, the longer night, and the boy curled up in my arms.

Death and destruction. Slivers of hope.

Kenji drove us to a remote location and used the last of his strength to make the tank invisible for most of the night; it was the only way we could wait out the battle and manage to sleep for a few hours. I'm still not sure how that guy is functioning. He's definitely way stronger than I've ever given him credit for.

The world around us is eerily calm. I shift a little and James is alert, up and asking questions the moment his mouth hinges open. His voice disturbs everyone, startling them awake. I use the back of my hand to rub at my eyes and adjust James in my lap, holding him close. I drop a kiss on the top of his head and tell him to be quiet.

"Why?" he asks.

I cover his mouth with my hand.

He slaps it away.

"Good morning, sunshine." Kenji blinks in our direction.

"Morning," I say back.

"I wasn't talking to you," he says, trying to smile. "I was talking to the sunshine."

I grin in response, not really sure where we're going with this. There's so much to talk about, and so much we don't want to talk about, that I don't know if we'll ever talk at all. I glance back at Castle and notice he's wide awake and staring out the window. I wave hello.

"Did you sleep all right?" I ask him.

Castle stares at me.

I glance at Kenji.

Kenji looks out the window, too.

I blow out a breath.

Everyone makes their way back to the present, slowly but surely. Once we're all in semiworking condition—Brendan and Winston included—Kenji doesn't waste any time.

"We have to figure out where we're going to go," he says. "We can't risk being on the road for too long, and I'm not sure how long or how well I'll be able to project. My energy is coming back, but slowly, and it's in and out. Not something I can rely on right now."

"We also need to think about food," Ian says groggily.

"Yeah, I'm pretty hungry," James adds.

I squeeze his shoulders. We're all starving.

"Right," Kenji says. "So does anyone have any ideas?"

Silence from all of us.

"Come on, guys," he says. "Think. Any hideouts, any secure spots—anywhere you've ever crashed that was once a safe space—"

"What about our old house?" James asks, looking around.

I sit up straighter, surprised I hadn't thought of it myself. "Right—of course," I say. "Good idea, James." I muss his hair. "That would work."

Kenji pounds his fist on the steering wheel. "Yes!" he says loudly. "Good. Excellent. Perfect. Thank God."

"But what if they come looking for us?" Lily asks. "Didn't Warner know about your old place?"

"Yeah," I tell her. "But if they think everyone from Omega Point is dead, they won't think to come search for me. Or any of us."

At that, the car goes dead quiet.

The elephant in the room has made an appearance, and now no one knows what to say. We all look to Castle for direction on how best to proceed, but he doesn't say a word. He's staring straight ahead at nothing at all, like he's been paralyzed from the inside.

"Let's go," Alia says quietly. She's the only one who responds to me, and she offers me a kind smile as she does. I decide I like her for it. "We should secure shelter as soon as possible. And maybe find James something to eat."

I beam at her. So touched that she would speak for James.

"Maybe we could find something all of us could eat," Ian cuts in, grumpy. I frown, but I can't blame him. My stomach has made a few protests of its own.

"We should have plenty of food back at the house," I say. "It's been paid for through the end of the year, so we'll have just about everything we need—water, electricity, a roof over our heads—but it'll be tight, and it'll be temporary. We'll have to come up with a more long-term solution soon."

"Sounds good," Kenji says to me. He turns back to look at everyone. "We all in agreement here?"

There's a murmur of consent and that's all we need, really, before we're off and heading back to my old place. Back to the beginning.

Relief floods through me.

I'm so grateful to be able to take James home. To let him sleep in his own bed. And though I know better than to ever say it out loud, a small part of me is happy that our time at Omega Point is officially over. There's a silver lining in all of this, and it's that Warner thinks we're all dead. And even though he's got Juliette now, he won't have her forever. She'll be safe until we can find a way to get her back, and until then, he won't come after us. We can find a way to live, away from all the violence and destruction.

Besides, I'm tired of fighting. I'm tired of being on the run and always having to risk my life and constantly worrying about James. I just want to go home. I want to take care of my brother. And I never, ever, *ever* want to feel what I felt last night.

I can't risk losing James, not ever again.

THIRTEEN

The roads are almost entirely abandoned. The sun is high and the wind is bitingly cold and though the rain has stopped, the air smells like snow, and I have a feeling it's going to be harsh. I wrap James more tightly in my arms, shivering against a chill coming from deep inside my body. He's fallen asleep again, his small face buried in the crook of my neck. I hug him closer to my chest.

With the opposition destroyed, there's no need to have many—if any—troops on the ground. They're probably clearing out the bodies now, cleaning up the mess and putting things back in order as soon as possible. It's what we always did.

Battle was necessary, but cleaning it up was just as crucial.

Warner used to drill that home: we were never to allow civilians time to grieve. We could never give them the opportunity to make martyrs of their loved ones. No, it was better for the deaths to seem as insignificant as possible.

Everyone had to go back to work right away.

So many times I was a part of those missions. I always hated Warner, hated The Reestablishment and all it stood for, but now I feel even more strongly about it all. Thinking

I'd lost James did something to me last night, and the damage is irreparable. I thought I knew what it was like to lose someone close to me, but I didn't, not really. Losing a parent is excruciating, but somehow, the pain is so much different from losing a child. And James, to me, in many ways, feels like my own kid. I raised him. Took care of him. Protected him. Fed him and clothed him. Taught him most everything he knows. He's my only hope in all this devastation—the one thing I've always lived for, always fought for. I'd be lost without him.

James gives my life purpose.

And I didn't realize this until last night.

What The Reestablishment does—separating parents from their children, separating spouses from each other, basically ripping families apart—they do it on purpose. And the cruelty of these actions hadn't really hit me until now.

I don't think I could ever be a part of something like that again.

FOURTEEN

We pull into the underground parking garage without a problem, and once we're inside, I can exhale. I know we'll be safe here.

The nine of us clamber out of the tank and stand around for a moment. Brendan and Winston are holding fast to each other, still recovering from their wounds. I'm not sure what happened to them, exactly, because no one is talking about it, but I don't think I want to know. Alia and Lily help Castle down from the tank, and Ian is close behind. Kenji is standing next to me. I'm still holding James in my arms, and I only put him down after he asks me to.

"You guys ready to go up?" I ask. "Shower? Eat some breakfast?"

"That sounds great, man," says Ian.

Everyone else agrees.

I lead the way, James clinging to my hand.

It's crazy—the last time we were here, we were on the run from Warner. Me and Juliette. It was the first time she met James, the first time it felt like we could really have a life together. And then Kenji showed up and redirected the course of everything. I shake my head, remembering. It feels like a million years ago, somehow. So much has changed. I was practically a different guy back then. I feel much older and harder and angrier now. Difficult to believe it was only a few months ago.

The front door is still messed up from when Warner and his guys busted it open, but we make do. I yank on the handle and then shove, hard, and the door swings inward.

Suddenly we're all crossing the threshold.

I'm looking around, amazed to see everything almost exactly the way we left it. A few things are knocked over and the place needs a serious cleaning, but it'll work. It'll be a great, safe place to live for a while. I start flipping switches and the small rooms flicker to life, fluorescent lights humming steadily in the silence. James bolts toward his bedroom, and I check the cabinets for canned goods and nonperishable items; we've still got tons of Saran-wrapped packages for the Automat.

I breathe a sigh of relief.

"Who wants breakfast?" I ask, holding up a few packets.

Kenji falls to his knees, shouting, "Hallelujah!" in the process; Ian practically tackles me. James comes racing out of his room shouting, "ME ME ME I DO I DO," and Lily laughs her head off. Alia smiles and leans against the wall as Brendan and Winston collapse on the couch, groaning in relief. Castle is the only one who remains silent.

"All right, everyone," Kenji says. "Adam and I will get the food going, and the rest of you can take turns washing up. Also, I hate to be super obvious here, but there's only one bathroom, and we all have to share, so let's please be aware of that. Adam's got some supplies, but not too much, so let's be frugal, okay? Let's remember we're living on rations now. Consideration is crucial."

There's general consent and lots of nodding, and everyone busies themselves with a different kind of preparation. Everyone except Castle, who sits down in the single armchair and doesn't move. He seems to be doing worse than Brendan and Winston, who happen to be in actual physical pain.

I'm still staring at the two of them when Ian slips away from the group to ask me if I have anything to help patch up Brendan and Winston. I assure him that I'll use whatever supplies I've got to fix them up as best I can. I always have a little medical kit at home, but it's not extensive, and I'm not a medic. But I know enough. I think I'll be able to help. This cheers up Ian significantly.

It's only once Kenji and I are busy preparing food in the kitchen that he brings up the most pressing issue. The one I'm still not sure how to resolve.

"So what are we going to do about Juliette?" Kenji asks, tossing an Automat packet into a bowl. "I'm already worried we waited this long to go after her."

I feel myself pale. I don't know how to tell him I had no immediate plans to go back out there. Certainly not to fight—not after what happened to James. "I don't know," I say. "I'm not sure what we can do."

Kenji stares at me, confused. "What do you mean? We have to get her out of there. Which means we have to *break* her out of there, which means we've got to plan another rescue mission." He shoots me a look. "I thought that was obvious."

I clear my throat. "But what about James? And Brendan and Winston? And Castle? We're not doing too well over here. Is it okay to just leave them here and—"

"Dude, what the hell are you talking about? Aren't you in love with this girl? Where's the fire under your ass? I thought you would be dying to get to her right now—"

"I am," I say urgently. "Of course I am. I'm just worried—it's so soon after they bombed Point that I just—"

"The longer we wait, the worse it's going to get." Kenji shakes his head. "We have to go as soon as possible. If we don't, she'll be stuck there forever, and Warner will use her as his torture monster. He'll probably kill her in the process without even meaning to."

I grip the edge of the counter and stare into the sink.

Shit.

Shit shit shit.

I spin around at the sound of James's voice, listen for a moment as he laughs at something Alia said. My heart constricts just *thinking* about walking away from him again. But I know I have a responsibility to Juliette. What would she do if I weren't there to help her? She needs me.

"Okay," I sigh. "Of course. What do we have to do?"

FIFTEEN

After breakfast, which was actually closer to lunch, I tend to Brendan and Winston for a bit, and set them up on the floor so they can get some proper rest. James and I had collected a decent stash of ratty blankets and pillows over the years, so there's just enough to go around, and thank God for that, because it's cold as hell. We even wrapped a blanket around Castle's shoulders. He's still barely moving, but we forced him to eat, so at least he's got a little color in his cheeks now.

With Brendan and Winston settled, Ian and Alia and Lily fed and comfortable, James safe and sound, and Castle resting, Kenji and I are finally ready to initiate some new plans.

"I'm going to go out," Kenji says. "Get on base and get nosy. Listen for rumors and whispers of what's going on—maybe even find Juliette, give her a heads-up that we're coming for her soon."

I nod. "That's a great start."

"Once I know more about what's going on, we can make a firm plan, scoop her up, and bring her home."

"So as soon as she's back," I say, "we'll have to move again."

"Probably, yeah."

I nod a few times. "Okay. All right." I swallow hard. "I'll wait here until you get back."

"Sounds good." Kenji grins, and then he's gone. Disappeared. The front door is yanked open and yanked closed, and I'm staring at the wall and trying not to freak out too much about what's going to happen next.

Another mission. Which means another chance to screw everything up and get ourselves killed. And then, if we're successful, we're rewarded with more running, more instability, more chaos.

I close my eyes.

I love Juliette. I really do. I want to help her and support her and be there for her. I want us to have a future together. But sometimes I wonder if it's ever going to happen.

This isn't easy to admit, but part of me doesn't want to put James at risk again—on the run again—for a girl who broke up with me. A girl who walked away from us.

I don't know what the right thing is anymore.

I don't know if my allegiance is to James or Juliette.

SIXTEEN

Kenji is back after only a couple of hours. His face ashen, his hands trembling. He's breathing hard and his eyes are unfocused and he sits down on the couch without a word and I'm already panicking.

"What happened?" I ask.

"What's going on?" Lily says.

"You okay, bro?" This from Ian.

We pepper him with questions and he doesn't answer. He stares, unblinking, a replica of Castle, who's sitting in a chair across from him.

Finally, after a long moment of silence, he speaks.

Three words.

"Juliette is dead."

Chaos.

Questions are flying and screams are muffled and everyone is shocked, horrified, freaking out.

I'm stunned.

My brain feels paralyzed, unwilling to process or digest this information. *Why?* I want to ask. *How?* How? How is it possible?

But I can't speak. I'm frozen in horror. Grief.

"It wasn't Warner who came after her," Kenji is saying,

tears falling fast down his face. "It was Anderson. Those were Anderson's men. They made the announcement just a couple hours ago," he says, choking on the words. "They said they bombed Omega Point, captured Juliette, and killed her just this morning. The supreme has already headed back to the capital."

"No," I gasp.

"We should've gone after her," Kenji is saying. "I should've stayed behind—I should've tried to find her—it's my fault," he says, hands in his hair, fighting back tears. "It's my fault she's dead. I should've gone after her—"

"It's not your fault," Ian says to him, rushing over and grabbing his arms. "Don't you dare put that on yourself."

"We lost a lot of people," Lily says. "People dear to us that we couldn't save. This is not your fault. I promise. We did our best."

Everyone is consoling Kenji now, trying to reassure him that there's no guilt necessary. No person to blame for all this.

But I can't agree.

I trip backward until I hit the wall, leaning against it for support. I know who to blame. I know where the fault lies.

Juliette is dead because of me.

JULIETTE'S JOURNAL

I keep thinking I need to stay calm, that it's all in my head, that everything is going to be fine and someone is going to open the door now, someone is going to let me out of here. I keep thinking it's going to happen. I keep thinking it has to happen, because things like this don't just happen. This doesn't happen. People aren't forgotten like this. Not abandoned like this.

This doesn't just happen.

My face is caked with blood from when they threw me on the ground and my hands are still shaking even as I write this. This pen is my only outlet, my only voice, because I have no one else to speak to, no mind but my own to drown in and all the lifeboats are taken and all the life preservers are broken and I don't know how to swim I can't swim I can't swim and it's getting so hard. It's getting so hard. It's like there are a million screams caught inside of my chest but I have to keep them all in because what's the point of screaming if you'll never be heard and no one will ever hear me in here. No one will ever hear me ever again.

I've learned to stare at things.

The walls. My hands. The cracks in the walls. The lines on my fingers. The shades of gray in the concrete. The shape of my finger-nails. I pick one thing and stare at it for what must be hours. I keep time in my head by counting the seconds as they pass. I keep days in my head by writing them down. Today is day two. Today is the second day. Today is a day.

Today.

It's so cold. It's so cold it's so cold.

Please please please

I started screaming today.

It's a strange thing, to never know peace. To know that no matter where you go, there is no sanctuary. That the threat of pain is always a whisper away. I'm not safe locked into these 4 walls, I was never safe leaving my house, and I couldn't even feel safe in the 14 years I lived at home. The asylum kills people every day, the world has already been taught to fear me, and my home is the same place where my father locked me in my room every night and my mother screamed at me for being the abomination she was forced to raise.

She always said it was my face.

There was something about my face, she said, that she couldn't stand. Something about my eyes, the way I looked at her, the fact that I even existed. She'd always tell me to stop looking at her. She'd always scream it. Like I might attack her. Stop looking at me, she'd scream. You just stop looking at me, she'd scream.

She put my hand in the fire once.

Just to see if it would burn, she said. Just to check if it was a regular hand, she said.

I was 6 years old then.

I remember because it was my birthday.

~~Am I insane yet?~~
~~Has it happened yet?~~
~~How will I ever know?~~

Sometimes I close my eyes and paint these walls a different color.

I imagine I'm wearing warm socks and sitting by a fire. I imagine someone's given me a book to read, a story to take me away from the torture of my own mind. I want to be someone else somewhere else with something else to fill my mind. I want to run, to feel the wind tug at my hair. I want to pretend that this is just a story within a story. That this cell is just a scene, that these hands don't belong to me, that this window leads to somewhere beautiful if only I could break it. I pretend this pillow is clean, I pretend this bed is soft. I pretend and pretend and pretend until the world becomes so breathtaking behind my eyelids that I can no longer contain it. But then my eyes fly open and I'm caught around the throat by a pair of hands that won't stop suffocating suffocating suffocating

My thoughts, I think, will soon be sound.

My mind, I hope, will soon be found.

I wonder what they're thinking. My parents. I wonder where they are. I wonder if they're okay now, if they're happy now, ~~if they finally got what they wanted.~~ I wonder if my mother will ever have another child. I wonder if someone will ever be kind enough to kill me and I wonder if hell is better than here. I wonder what my face looks like now. I wonder if I'll ever breathe fresh air again.

I wonder about so many things.

Sometimes I'll stay awake for days just counting everything I can find. I count the walls, the cracks in the walls, my fingers and toes. I count the springs in the bed, the threads in the blanket, the steps it takes to cross the room and back. I count my teeth and the individual *hairs on my head and the number of seconds I can hold my breath.*

But sometimes I get so tired that I forget I'm not allowed to wish for things anymore and I find myself wishing for the one thing I've always wanted. The only thing I've always dreamt about.

I wish all the time for a friend.

I dream about it. I imagine what it would be like. To smile and be smiled upon. To have a person to confide in, someone who wouldn't throw things at me or stick my hands in the fire or beat me for being born. Someone who would hear that I'd been thrown away and would try to find me, who would never be afraid of me.

Someone who'd know I'd never try to hurt them.

I fold myself into a corner of this room and bury my head in my knees and rock back and forth and back and forth and back and forth and I wish and I wish and I wish and I dream of impossible things until I've cried myself to sleep.

I wonder what it would be like to have a friend.

And then I wonder who else is locked in this asylum. I wonder where the other screams are coming from.

I wonder if they're coming from me.

~~*There's something simmering inside of me.*~~

~~*Something I've never dared to tap into, something I'm afraid to acknowledge. There's a part of me clawing to break free from the cage I've trapped it in, banging on the doors of my heart begging to be free.*~~

~~*Begging to let go.*~~

~~*Every day I feel like I'm reliving the same nightmare. I open my mouth to shout, to fight, to swing my fists but my vocal chords are*~~

~~out, my arms are heavy and weighted down as if trapped in wet~~
~~cement and I'm screaming but no one can hear me, no one can reach~~
~~me and I'm caught. And it's killing me.~~

~~I've always had to make myself submissive, subservient, twisted~~
~~into a pleading, passive mop just to make everyone else feel safe and~~
~~comfortable. My existence has become a fight to prove I'm harmless,~~
~~that I'm not a threat, that I'm capable of living among other human~~
~~beings without hurting them.~~

~~And I'm so tired I'm so tired I'm so tired I'm so tired and some-~~
~~times I get so angry~~

I don't know what's happening to me.

We had homes. Before.

All different kinds.

1-story homes. 2-story homes. 3-story homes.

We bought lawn ornaments and twinkle lights, learned to ride bikes without training wheels. We purchased lives confined within 1, 2, 3 stories already built, stories caught inside of structures we could not change.

We lived in those stories for a while.

We followed the tale laid out for us, the prose pinned down in every square foot of space we'd acquired. We were content with the plot twists that only mildly redirected our lives. We signed on the dotted line for the things we didn't know we cared about. We ate the things we shouldn't, spent money when we couldn't, lost sight of the Earth we had to inhabit, and wasted wasted wasted everything. Food. Water. Resources.

Soon the skies were gray with chemical pollution and the

plants and animals were sick from genetic modification, and diseases rooted themselves in our air, our meals, our blood and bones. The food disappeared. The people were dying. Our empire fell to pieces.

The Reestablishment said they would help us. Save us. Rebuild our society.

Instead they tore us all apart.

I'm sorry. I'm so sorry. I'm so sorry I'm so sorry I'm so so sorry I'm so sorry. I'm so sorry I'm so sorry I'm so so sorry. I'm so sorry. I'm so sorry. I'm so sorry I'm so so sorry I'm so sorry I'm so sorry I'm so sorry I'm so so sorry. I'm so sorry. I'm so sorry I'm so sorry I'm so so sorry I'm so sorry. I'm so sorry. I'm so sorry I'm so so sorry. I'm so sorry. I'm so sorry I'm so sorry I'm so so sorry I'm so sorry. I'm so sorry I'm so sorry. I'm so so sorry. I'm so sorry. I'm so sorry I'm so sorry I'm so so sorry I'm so sorry. I'm so sorry. I'm so sorry I'm so so sorry. I'm sorry I'm so sorry please forgive me.

It was an accident.

Forgive me

Please forgive me

Swallow the tears back often enough and they'll start feeling like acid dripping down your throat.

It's that terrible moment when you're sitting still so still so still because ~~you don't want them to see you cry~~ you don't want to cry but your lips won't stop trembling and your eyes are filled to the brim with please *and* I beg you *and* please *and* I'm sorry *and* please *and* have mercy *and* maybe this time it'll be different *but it's* always the same. There's no one to run to for comfort. No one on your side.

Light a candle for me, I used to whisper to no one.

Someone

Anyone

If you're out there

Please tell me you can feel this fire.

These letters are all I have left.

26 friends to tell my stories to.

26 letters are all I need. I can stitch them together to create oceans and ecosystems. I can fit them together to form planets and solar systems. I can use letters to construct skyscrapers and metropolitan cities populated by people, places, things, and ideas that are more real to me than these 4 walls.

I need nothing but letters to live. Without them I would not exist.

Because these words I write down are the only proof I have that I'm still alive.

Sometimes I think the shadows are moving.

Sometimes I think someone might be watching.

Sometimes this idea scares me and sometimes the idea makes me so absurdly happy I can't stop crying. And then sometimes I think I have no idea when I started losing my mind in here. Nothing seems real anymore and I can't tell if I'm screaming out loud or only in my head.

There's no one here to hear me.

To tell me I'm not dead.

***

No one wants a dandelion.

They crop up all over the place, ugly and unfortunate, an average blossom in a world desperately seeking beauty. They're weeds, people say. They're uninteresting and offer no fragrance and there are too many of them, too much of them, we don't want them, destroy them.

Dandelions are a nuisance.

We desire the buttercups, the daffodils, the morning glories. We want the azalea, the poinsettia, the calla lily. We pluck them from our gardens and plant them in our homes and we don't seem to remember their toxic nature.

We don't seem to care that

if you get too close?

if you take a small bite?

The beauty is replaced with pain and laced with a poison that laughs in your blood, destroys your organs, infects your heart.

But pick a dandelion.

Pick a dandelion and make a salad, eat the leaves, the flower, the stem. Thread it in your hair, plant it in the ground and watch it thrive.

Pick a dandelion and close your eyes

make a wish

blow it into the wind.

Watch it

change

the
world.

Hate.

    It's poison, an unrelenting punch to the gut, an injustice injected directly into your bloodstream that slowly paralyzes your organs until you can't breathe
    you can't
    breathe
    because loneliness has stuffed itself into your clothes and you're rotting to death in a dark corner of the world and you're already forgotten.
    You never even were.

Pick a cloud just to pin it down and wear it in your hair.
    Jump up to catch its soft soft strands, its feathery wisps; piles of tufted snow sailing through the air, cotton candy stretched so thin it melts the moment you try to taste it.
    Life is like a cloud.
    It comes in a million shapes and sizes and it offers no guarantees, no certainties, no sympathies for the man who told his kid he'd fly a kite today, no consideration for the girl who was sure she'd see the sun today, no promises for the weary world and the wants wants wants of which it has too many today.
    Life is like that.
    Sometimes full and fluffy and floating along and sometimes dark and angry and sobbing sobbing sobbing anger and passion and

vengeance and retaliation.

    It's agony

    It's anguish

    It's a gift, a lesson, a reminder.

    Because only once the storm has passed, only once the tears have flooded the rivers and gorged the ground and washed away the dirt the debris the destruction and decay, only then—

    only then will the sun step outside

    smile to the sky

    and dare to shine.

I count everything.

    Even numbers, odd numbers, multiples of ten. I count the ticks of the clock I count the tocks of the clock I count the lines between the lines on a sheet of paper. I count the broken beats of my heart I count my pulse and my blinks and the number of tries it takes to inhale enough oxygen for my lungs. I stay like this I stand like this I count like this until the feeling stops. Until the tears stop spilling, until my fists stop shaking, until my heart stops aching.

    There are never enough numbers.

Loneliness is a strange sort of thing.

    It creeps up on you, quiet and still, sits by your side in the dark, strokes your hair as you sleep. It wraps itself around your bones, squeezing so tight you almost can't breathe, almost can't hear the pulse racing in your blood as it rushes up your skin and touches its lips to the soft hairs at the back of your neck. It leaves lies in your heart, lies next to you at night, leeches the light out from every corner. It's a constant companion, clasping your hand only to yank you down when you're struggling to stand up, catching your tears only to force them down your throat. It scares you simply by standing by your side.

You wake up in the morning and wonder who you are. You fail to fall asleep at night and tremble in your skin. You doubt you doubt you doubt

do I

don't I

should I

why won't I

And even when you're ready to let go. When you're ready to break free. When you're ready to be brand-new. Loneliness is an old friend standing beside you in the mirror, looking you in the eye, challenging you to live your life without it. You can't find the words to fight yourself, to fight the words screaming that you're not enough never enough never ever enough.

Loneliness is a bitter, wretched companion.

Sometimes it just won't let go.

I am a thief.

I stole this notebook and this pen from one of the doctors, from one of his lab coats when he wasn't looking, and I shoved them both down my pants. This was just before he ordered those men to come and get me. The ones in the strange suits with the thick gloves and the gas masks with the foggy plastic windows hiding their eyes. They were aliens, I remember thinking. I remember thinking they must've been aliens because they couldn't have been human, the ones who

189

handcuffed my hands behind my back, the ones who strapped me to my seat. They stuck Tasers to my skin over and over for no reason other than to hear me scream but I wouldn't. I whimpered but I never said a word. I felt the tears streak down my cheeks but I wasn't crying.

I think it made them angry.

They slapped me awake even though my eyes were open when we arrived. Someone unstrapped me without removing my handcuffs and kicked me in both kneecaps before ordering me to rise. And I tried. I tried but I couldn't and finally 6 hands shoved me out the door and my face was bleeding on the concrete for a while. I can't really remember the part where they dragged me inside.

I feel cold all the time.

I feel empty, like there is nothing inside of me but this broken heart, the only organ left in this shell. I feel the bleats echo within me, I feel the thumping reverberate around my skeleton. I have a heart, says science, but I am a monster, says society. And I know it, of course I know it. I know what I've done. I'm not asking for sympathy.

But sometimes I think—sometimes I wonder—if I were a monster—surely, I would feel it by now?

I would feel angry and vicious and vengeful. I'd know blind rage and bloodlust and a need for vindication.

Instead I feel an abyss within me that's so deep, so dark I can't see within it; I can't see what it holds. I do not know what I am or what might happen to me.

I do not know what I might do again.

***

I sit here every day.

~~174~~ 175 days I've sat here so far.

Some days I stand up and stretch and feel these stiff bones, these creaky joints, this trampled spirit cramped inside my being. I roll my shoulders, I blink my eyes, I count the seconds creeping up the walls, the minutes shivering under my skin, the breaths I have to remember to take. Sometimes I allow my mouth to drop open, just a little bit; I touch my tongue to the backs of my teeth and the seam of my lips and I walk around this small space, I trail my fingers along the cracks in the concrete and wonder, I wonder what it would be like to speak out loud and be heard. I hold my breath, listen closely for anything, any sound of life, and wonder at the beauty, the impossibility of possibly hearing another person breathing beside me.

I stop. I stand still. I close my eyes and try to remember a world beyond these walls. I wonder what it would be like to know that I'm not dreaming, that this isolated existence is not caged within my own mind.

And I do. I do I wonder, I think about it all the time.

What it would be like to kill myself.

Because I never really know, I still can't tell the difference, I'm never quite certain whether or not I'm actually alive.

So I sit here.

I sit here every day.

Run, I said to myself.

Run until your lungs collapse, until the wind whips and snaps at your tattered clothes, until you're a blur that blends into the back-ground.

Run, Juliette, run faster, run until your bones break and your shins split and your muscles atrophy and your heart dies because it was always too big for your chest and it beat too fast for too long and run.

Run run run until you can't hear their feet behind you. Run until they drop their fists and their shouts dissolve in the air. Run with your eyes open and your mouth shut and dam the river rushing up behind your eyes. Run, Juliette.

Run until you drop dead.

Make sure your heart stops before they ever reach you. Before they ever touch you.

Run, I said.

Just a moment.

Just one second, just one more minute, just give me another hour or maybe the weekend to think it over it's not so much it's not so hard it's all we ever ask for it's a simple request.

But the moments the seconds the minutes the hours the days and years become one big mistake, one extraordinary opportunity slipped right through our fingers because we couldn't decide, we couldn't understand, we needed more time, we didn't know what to do.

We don't even know what we've done.

We have no idea how we even got here when all we ever wanted was to wake up in the morning and go to sleep at night and maybe stop for ice cream on the way home and that one decision, that one choice, that one accidental opportunity unraveled everything we've ever known and ever believed in and what do we do?

What do we do
from here?

On the darkest days you have to search for a spot of brightness, on the coldest days you have to seek out a spot of warmth; on the bleakest days you have to keep your eyes onward and upward and on the saddest days you have to leave them open to let them cry. To then let them dry. To give them a chance to wash out the pain in order to see fresh and clear once again.

Nothing in this life will ever make sense to me but I can't help but try to collect the change and hope it's enough to pay for our mistakes.

~~*I am not insane. I*~~

~~am not insane. I am not insane. I am not insane. I am not insane. I~~
~~am not insane. I am not insane. I am not insane. I am not insane. I~~
~~am not insane. I am not insane. I am not insane. I am not insane. I~~
~~am not insane. I am not insane. I am not insane. I am not insane. I~~
~~am not insane. I am not insane. I am not insane. I am not insane. I~~
~~am not insane. I am not insane. I am not insane. I am not insane. I~~
~~am not insane. I am not insane. I am not insane. I am not insane. I~~
~~am not insane. I am not insane. I am not insane. I am not insane. I~~
~~am not insane. I am not insane. I am not insane. I am not insane. I~~
~~am not insane.~~ I am not insane.

I don't know when it started.

I don't know why it started.

I don't know anything about anything except for the screaming.

My mother screaming when she realized she could no longer touch me. My father screaming when he realized what I'd done to my mother. My parents screaming when they'd lock me in my room and tell me I should be grateful. For their food. For their humane treatment of this thing that could not possibly be their child. For the yardstick they used to measure the distance I needed to keep away.

I ruined their lives, is what they said to me.

I stole their happiness. Destroyed my mother's hope for ever having children again.

Couldn't I see what I'd done? *is what they'd ask me.* Couldn't I see that I'd ruined everything?

I tried so hard to fix what I'd ruined. I tried every single day to be what they wanted. I tried all the time to be better but I never really knew how.

I only know now that the scientists are wrong.

The world is flat.

I know because I was tossed right off the edge and I've been trying to hold on for seventeen years. I've been trying to climb back up for seventeen years but it's nearly impossible to beat gravity when no one is willing to give you a hand.

When no one wants to risk touching you.

One word, two lips, three four five fingers form one fist.

One corner, two parents, three four five reasons to hide.

One child, two eyes, three four seventeen years of fear.

A broken broomstick, a pair of wild faces, angry whispers, locks on my door.

Look at me, is what I wanted to say to you. Talk to me every once in a while. Find me a cure for these tears, I'd really like to exhale for the first time in my life.

The broken broomstick was the mediator between me and them.

The broomstick broke on my back.

I remember televisions and fireplaces and porcelain sinks. I remember movie tickets and parking lots and SUVs. I remember hair salons and holidays and window shutters and dandelions and the smell of freshly paved driveways. I remember toothpaste commercials and ladies in high heels and old men in business suits. I remember mailmen and libraries and boy bands and balloons and Christmas trees.

I remember being 10 years old when we couldn't ignore the food shortages anymore and things got so expensive no one could afford to live.

Why don't you just kill yourself? *someone at school asked me once.*

I think it was the kind of question intended to be cruel, but it was the first time I'd ever contemplated the possibility. I didn't know what to say. Maybe I was crazy to consider it, but I'd always hoped that if I were a good enough girl—if I did everything right, if I said the right things or said nothing at all—I thought my parents would change their minds. I thought they would finally listen when I tried to talk. I thought they would give me a chance. I thought they might finally love me.

I always had that ~~stupid~~ hope.

There's no light in here. I'm not sure if I'm writing on paper or skin or stone but

Were you happy

Were you sad

Were you scared

Were you mad

the first time you screamed?

Were you fighting for your life your decency your dignity your humanity

When someone touches you now, do you scream?

When someone smiles at you now, do you smile back?

Did he tell you not to scream did he hit you when you cried?

Did he have one nose two eyes two lips two cheeks two ears two eyebrows.

Was he one human who looked just like you.

Color your personality.
Shapes and sizes are variety.
Your heart is an anomaly.
Your actions
are
the
only
traces
you leave
behind.

Hang tight
    Hold on
    Look up
    Stay strong
    Hang on
    Hold tight
    Look strong
    Stay up
    One day I might break
    One day I might
    b r e a k
    free

Don't miss the epic conclusion to the
New York Times bestselling SHATTER ME series.

ONE

I am an hourglass.

My seventeen years have collapsed and buried me from the inside out. My legs feel full of sand and stapled together, my mind overflowing with grains of indecision, choices unmade and impatient as time runs out of my body. The small hand of a clock taps me at one and two, three and four, whispering hello, get up, stand up, it's time to

wake up

wake up

"Wake up," he whispers.

A sharp intake of breath and I'm awake but not up, surprised but not scared, somehow staring into the very desperately green eyes that seem to know too much, too well. Aaron Warner Anderson is bent over me, his worried eyes inspecting me, his hand caught in the air like he might've been about to touch me.

He jerks back.

He stares, unblinking, chest rising and falling.

"Good morning," I assume. I'm unsure of my voice, of the hour and this day, of these words leaving my lips and this body that contains me.

I notice he's wearing a white button-down, half untucked

into his curiously unrumpled black slacks. His shirtsleeves are folded, pushed up past his elbows.

His smile looks like it hurts.

I pull myself into a seated position and Warner shifts to accommodate me. I have to close my eyes to steady the sudden dizziness, but I force myself to remain still until the feeling passes.

I'm tired and weak from hunger, but other than a few general aches, I seem to be fine. I'm alive. I'm breathing and blinking and feeling human and I know exactly why.

I meet his eyes. "You saved my life."

I was shot in the chest.

Warner's father put a bullet in my body and I can still feel the echoes of it. If I focus, I can relive the exact moment it happened; the pain: so intense, so excruciating; I'll never be able to forget it.

I suck in a startled breath.

I'm finally aware of the familiar foreignness of this room and I'm quickly seized by a panic that screams I did not wake up where I fell asleep. My heart is racing and I'm inching away from him, hitting my back against the headboard, clutching at these sheets, trying not to stare at the chandelier I remember all too well—

"It's okay—" Warner is saying. "It's all right—"

"What am I doing here?" Panic, panic; terror clouds my consciousness. "Why did you bring me here again—?"

"Juliette, please, I'm not going to hurt you—"

"Then why did you bring me here?" My voice is starting

to break and I'm struggling to keep it steady. "Why bring me back to this *hellhole*—"

"I had to hide you." He exhales, looks up at the wall.

"What? Why?"

"No one knows you're alive." He turns to look at me. "I had to get back to base. I needed to pretend everything was back to normal and I was running out of time."

I force myself to lock away the fear.

I study his face and analyze his patient, earnest tone. I remember him last night—it must've been last night—I remember his face, remember him lying next to me in the dark. He was tender and kind and gentle and he saved me, saved my life. Probably carried me into bed. Tucked me in beside him. It must've been him.

But when I glance down at my body I realize I'm wearing clean clothes, no blood or holes or anything anywhere and I wonder who washed me, wonder who changed me, and worry that might've been Warner, too.

"Did you . . ." I hesitate, touching the hem of the shirt I'm wearing. "Did—I mean—my clothes—"

He smiles. He stares until I'm blushing and I decide I hate him a little and then he shakes his head. Looks into his palms. "No," he says. "The girls took care of that. I just carried you to bed."

"The girls," I whisper, dazed.

The girls.

Sonya and Sara. They were there too, the healer twins, they helped Warner. They helped him save me because he's the only one who can touch me now, the only person in the world who'd have been able to transfer their healing power safely into my body.

My thoughts are on fire.

Where are the girls what happened to the girls and where is Anderson and the war and oh God what's happened to Adam and Kenji and Castle and I have to get up I have to get up I have to get up and get out of bed and get going

but

I try to move and Warner catches me. I'm off-balance, unsteady; I still feel as though my legs are anchored to this bed and I'm suddenly unable to breathe, seeing spots and feeling faint. Need up. Need out.

Can't.

"Warner." My eyes are frantic on his face. "What happened? What's happening with the battle—?"

"Please," he says, gripping my shoulders. "You need to start slowly; you should eat something—"

"Tell me—"

"Don't you want to eat first? Or shower?"

"No," I hear myself say. "I have to know now."

One moment. Two and three.

Warner takes a deep breath. A million more. Right hand over left, spinning the jade ring on his pinkie finger over and over and over and over "It's over," he says.

"What?"

I say the word but my lips make no sound. I'm numb, somehow. Blinking and seeing nothing.

6

"It's over," he says again.

"No."

I exhale the word, exhale the impossibility.

He nods. He's disagreeing with me.

"No."

"Juliette."

"No," I say. "No. No. Don't be stupid," I say to him. "Don't be ridiculous," I say to him. *"Don't lie to me goddamn you,"* but now my voice is high and broken and shaking and "No," I gasp, "no, no, *no—*"

I actually stand up this time. My eyes are filling fast with tears and I blink and blink but the world is a mess and I want to laugh because all I can think is how horrible and beautiful it is, that our eyes blur the truth when we can't bear to see it.

The ground is hard.

I know this to be an actual fact because it's suddenly pressed against my face and Warner is trying to touch me but I think I scream and slap his hands away because I already know the answer. I must already know the answer because I can feel the revulsion bubbling up and unsettling my insides but I ask anyway. I'm horizontal and somehow still tipping over and the holes in my head are tearing open and I'm staring at a spot on the carpet not ten feet away and I'm not sure I'm even alive but I have to hear him say it.

"Why?" I ask.

It's just a word, stupid and simple.

"Why is the battle over?" I ask. I'm not breathing

anymore, not really speaking at all; just expelling letters through my lips.

Warner is not looking at me.

He's looking at the wall and at the floor and at the bed-sheets and at the way his knuckles look when he clenches his fists but no not at me he won't look at me and his next words are so, so soft.

"Because they're dead, love. They're all dead."

TWO

My body locks.

My bones, my blood, my brain freeze in place, seizing in some kind of sudden, uncontrollable paralysis that spreads through me so quickly I can't seem to breathe. I'm wheezing in deep, strained inhalations, and the walls won't stop swaying in front of me.

Warner pulls me into his arms.

"Let go of me," I scream, but, oh, only in my imagination because my lips are finished working and my heart has just expired and my mind has gone to hell for the day and my eyes my eyes I think they're bleeding. Warner is whispering words of comfort I can't hear and his arms are wrapped entirely around me, trying to keep me together through sheer physical force but it's no use.

I feel nothing.

Warner is shushing me, rocking me back and forth, and it's only then that I realize I'm making the most excruciating, earsplitting sound, agony ripping through me. I want to speak, to protest, to accuse Warner, to blame him, to call him a liar, but I can say nothing, can form nothing but sounds so pitiful I'm almost ashamed of myself. I break free of his arms, gasping and doubling over, clutching my stomach.

"Adam." I choke on his name.

"Juliette, please—"

"Kenji." I'm hyperventilating into the carpet now.

"Please, love, let me help you—"

"What about James?" I hear myself say. "He was left at Omega Point—he wasn't a-allowed to c-come—"

"It's all been destroyed," Warner says slowly, quietly. "Everything. They tortured some of your members into giving away the exact location of Omega Point. Then they bombed the entire thing."

"Oh, *God*." I cover my mouth with one hand and stare, unblinking, at the ceiling.

"I'm so sorry," he says. "You have no idea how sorry I am."

"Liar," I whisper, venom in my voice. I'm angry and mean and I can't be bothered to care. "You're not sorry at all."

I glance at Warner just long enough to see the hurt flash in and out of his eyes. He clears his throat.

"I am sorry," he says again, quiet but firm. He picks up his jacket from where it was hanging on a nearby rack; shrugs it on without a word.

"Where are you going?" I ask, guilty in an instant.

"You need time to process this and you clearly have no use for my company. I will attend to a few tasks until you're ready to talk."

"Please tell me you're wrong." My voice breaks. My breath catches. "Tell me there's a chance you could be wrong—"

Warner stares at me for what feels like a long time. "If

there were even the slightest chance I could spare you this pain," he finally says, "I would've taken it. You must know I wouldn't have said it if it weren't absolutely true."

And it's *this*—his sincerity—that finally snaps me in half.

Because the truth is so unbearable I wish he'd spare me a lie.

I don't remember when Warner left.

I don't remember how he left or what he said. All I know is that I've been lying here curled up on the floor long enough. Long enough for the tears to turn to salt, long enough for my throat to dry up and my lips to chap and my head to pound as hard as my heart.

I sit up slowly, feel my brain twist somewhere in my skull. I manage to climb onto the bed and sit there, still numb but less so, and pull my knees to my chest.

Life without Adam.

Life without Kenji, without James and Castle and Sonya and Sara and Brendan and Winston and all of Omega Point. My friends, all destroyed with the flick of a switch.

Life without Adam.

I hold on tight, pray the pain will pass.

It doesn't.

Adam is gone.

My first love. My first friend. My only friend when I had none and now he's gone and I don't know how I feel. Strange, mostly. Delirious, too. I feel empty and broken and cheated and guilty and angry and desperately, desperately sad.

We'd been growing apart since escaping to Omega Point, but that was my fault. He wanted more from me, but I wanted him to live a long life. I wanted to protect him from the pain I would cause him. I tried to forget him, to move on without him, to prepare myself for a future separate and apart from him.

I thought staying away would keep him alive.

Stupid girl.

The tears are fresh and falling fast now, traveling quietly down my cheeks and into my open, gasping mouth. My shoulders won't stop shaking and my fists keep clenching and my body is cramping and my knees are knocking and old habits are crawling out of my skin and I'm counting cracks and colors and sounds and shudders and rocking back and forth and back and forth and back and forth and I have to let him go I have to let him go I have to I have to

I close my eyes

and *breathe*.

Harsh, hard, rasping breaths.

In.

Out.

Count them.

I've been here before, I tell myself. I've been lonelier than this, more hopeless than this, more desperate than this. I've been here before and I survived. I can get through this.

But never have I been so thoroughly robbed. Love and possibility, friendships and futures: gone. I have to start over now; face the world alone again. I have to make one final choice: give up or go on.

So I get to my feet.

My head is spinning, thoughts knocking into one another, but I swallow back the tears. I clench my fists and try not to scream and I tuck my friends in my heart and

revenge

I think

has never looked so sweet.